For Heather Carter,
who has learned to choose
her battles so well

FOCUS ON THE FAMILY®

The Struggle

Nancy Rue

BETHANY HOUSE PUBLISHERS
MINNEAPOLIS, MINNESOTA 55438

Focus on the Family books are available at special quantity discounts when
purchased in bulk by corporations, organizations, churches, or groups.
Special imprints, messages, and excerpts can be produced to meet your needs.
For more information, contact: Resource Sales Group, Focus on the Family,
8605 Explorer Drive, Colorado Springs, CO 80920; or phone (800) 932-9123.

A Focus on the Family book
Published by Bethany House Publishers
A Ministry of Bethany Fellowship International
11400 Hampshire Avenue South
Bloomington, Minnesota 55438
www.bethanyhouse.com

Printed in the United States of America by
Bethany Press International, Bloomington, Minnesota 55438

Library of Congress Cataloging-in-Publication Data

Rue, Nancy N.
    The struggle / Nancy N. Rue.
        p. cm. — (Christian Heritage series. The Santa Fe years ; 5)
Summary: As Germany surrenders and victory in Europe is declared, eleven-
year-old Will begins to understand what things are worth fighting for and
what things are better left to God.
    ISBN 1-56179-895-9
1. World War, 1939-1945—United States—Juvenile fiction. [1. World War,
1939-1945—United States—Fiction. 2. Santa Fe (N.M.)—History—20th
century—Fiction. 3. Christian life—Fiction.] I. Title.
    PZ7.R88515 Sve   2002
    [Fic]—dc21   2002000064

02 03 04 05 06 07 08 / 14 13 12 11 10 9 8 7 6 5 4 3 2 1

S o help me, Will Hutchinson, if I have to drag this stupid wagon one more inch, I'm gonna jump somebody, and it's probably gonna be you!"

Fawn dropped the handle of the Radio Flyer wagon and let it fall with a metal clank to the sidewalk in front of Woolworth's. She folded her arms so hard against her chest, Will was surprised she didn't knock the air right out of herself. He would have laughed, if he hadn't learned a long time ago that it was a good idea to take Fawn's threats seriously.

"Come on, Fawn," he said, taking a step backward. "It's for the war effort. General Eisenhower says—"

"I don't care what some old general says! I'm sick of picking up stuff people were gonna throw *away* and hauling it around in this dumb wagon."

"It's just waste paper, Fawn," Will said. "It's not like it's garbage or something. And Eisenhower isn't just 'some old general.' " Will took a breath and switched to his smart voice. "He's the Supreme Allied Commander of all the armed forces in

Europe, and he says if we keep saving stuff like paper and tires and all, we can keep the soldiers supplied and win the war."

"I'm sick of the *war*, too," Fawn said, her black eyes snapping. She was getting close to clobbering him, Will could tell.

"So who isn't?" he said. "But if we don't win it, we're gonna have to *keep* bein' sick of it." He could feel the snapping in his own blue eyes. "So pick up that handle and let's move. We got about 20 more stores to go to."

It obviously sounded like 20 too many for Fawn. She flew at Will, knocking him off balance and tumbling both of them to the sidewalk. They rolled down the bricks, past the curio shop and the jewelers', finally coming to a stop in front of Rexall Drugs.

Will shoved Fawn off of him and looked up to see Miguel and Abe looking down at him. Big Abe was wearing his usual bewildered expression. He was as large as Will, Fawn, and Miguel put together, but although he had four years on their 11 and 12, he would never get too far past 6 in his mind. His foster parents, Reverend Bud and Tina, said that was what made him special.

Miguel, on the other hand, though not much bigger than the wiry Fawn, was probably the sharpest tack in the box. At least, that was what Will had heard grown-ups say. And right now, his dark Spanish eyes were flashing a message: *You're making a spectacle of yourself! Get up!*

Will scrambled to his feet and brushed the brick dust off of his dungarees. Miguel put a hand down for Fawn, but she slapped it aside and stood up on her own. Although she glared at Will, she didn't have her fists doubled up. For the moment, at least, it appeared she had gotten all of her mad out.

"We do not have time for all of this fooling around," Miguel said in his always-proper grammar. English was his second language, but Will had thought many times that he spoke it better than most people who had been speaking it since age two. "We still have much to do."

"Much," Abe said, bobbing his head of butter-blond hair.

"It's three against one, Fawn," Will said. "And besides—" He wiggled his eyebrows so they tickled against the shock of on-the-brown-side-of-blond hair that fell over his forehead. "Mom gave me money for us to have a malt at the Plaza when we're done."

Abe's round hazel eyes lit up, and Miguel's face broke into a slice of a grin.

"Why didn't you say so?" Fawn said. "What are we lollygagging around here for—let's go!"

She snatched up the wagon handle and took off across San Francisco Street to the park in the center of Santa Fe's Plaza, with Abe, Miguel, and Will on her heels. They took one of the four paths that cut the park's grass into quarters and headed for Hinkle's Store on the east side. The cottonwoods that hovered over the square like parents were just getting their spring leaves, and they cast speckled shadows on the kids as they ran. It felt happy to Will, and he savored it, the way he would a big wad of bubble gum. After all, happy moments weren't coming along as often as they used to.

But we're gonna get a ton *of paper for General Eisenhower's Waste Paper Campaign,* he told himself, *and that's gonna help end the war and then Dad'll come home and we'll be happy all the time—*

"Okay—" Fawn was shouting from the corner. "First we hit Hinkle's, and then Guarantee Shoes, and then the Thunderbird Curio Shop."

"Then malt!" Abe cried. He was grinning so big, Will could see little beads of spit at the corners of his mouth.

I don't think I'm ever that *happy,* Will thought.

"No," Will said. "After the Thunderbird, we go to the train office, then we go to all the stores on the west side of the Plaza, *then* we get a malt."

"I would not push it, my friend," Miguel murmured to him.

Fawn's eyes were narrowed down so far her face was practically coming to a point.

"Oh, all right," Will said. "After the curio shop we get a malt, *then* we do the west side—"

He was sure Fawn didn't hear any of that. She and Abe were already dodging cars as they crossed the street, wagon in tow. Miguel waited for Will.

"You are thinking today," he said.

"I think every day," Will said.

"But today, your thoughts are deep."

If it had been anybody else, Will would have told him he was a goof. But it was Miguel. He had a way of seeing things that everyone else missed.

"Yeah," Will said. "I'm thinkin' how everybody wants to give up on the war effort—not just Fawn."

Miguel nodded as his eyes drifted toward the half-full wagon, which had by now made it safely to the corner.

"People have not been generous today," he said.

"I don't get it. Don't they *want* the war to be over? They must not have people over there fighting, that's all I got to say."

Will's voice trailed off. Miguel was looking at the ground.

Aw, man, Will thought. *I really* am *a goof.*

Miguel, Will knew, didn't need anyone to remind him that he didn't have anybody over there fighting. His father had died on the same Death March in Bataan in the Philippines that had made Will's father a prisoner of war. Will could believe that his father was still alive in the prison camp. Miguel had no such hope.

Will straightened up to his full height, so that he was a head taller than Miguel.

"Let's go remind people there's still a war on," he said. "We don't want it so all those guys died for nothin', right?"

To his relief, Miguel smiled, and the two of them crossed the street to the spot where Abe and Fawn were waiting impatiently.

"Could you fellas get the lead outa your feet?" Fawn said.

Abe nodded and muttered, "Malt. Chocolate."

"Keep your shirt on, big guy," Will said. "We gotta get this wagon loaded up."

He nodded to Fawn to pull the wagon up under the striped awning that hung over Hinkle's, shielding its display window from the glaring afternoon sun. Even in March, it was bright enough to make a person squint.

"I hope we get to talk to Mr. Hinkle himself," Will said. "He'll probably give us a whole *bunch* of stuff."

Just then the door opened with the jangling of the bell that hung from it, and a woman stepped out with a shopping bag. A man stood in the doorway waving to her, and Will recognized him as one of Mr. Hinkle's salesmen. He'd escorted Will's mother to the door a couple of times when Will had gone shopping with her. He smiled constantly, as if he put on his grin with his clothes in the morning.

But when the man's eyes fell on the group with the wagon, the smile turned suspicious.

"You weren't planning to bring that vehicle in here, were you?" he said.

"What vehicle?" Fawn said. "We don't have no 'vehicle.' "

"*Any* vehicle," Miguel said softly.

The man pointed to the wagon. "Looks like a vehicle to me."

And you *look like a Percy Pants to me,* Will thought. *What is that you're dolled up in?*

The man wore a striped polo shirt and wide-legged dungarees that appeared to be belted far too high. The entire getup made him look as if his legs were coming directly out of his chin. The fact that his head was small and seemed to wobble on a long, thin neck gave him the appearance of a character in a child's drawing. If he hadn't been looking at the wagon with such a sour expression, Will might have laughed.

"We're collecting paper for the General Eisenhower Waste Paper Campaign," Will said quickly, before Fawn could say anything more and really mess it up. "Mr. Hinkle always gives us—"

"Do I look like Mr. Hinkle to you?" the man said.

"Well, no, you don't," Will said, forcing himself not to add that Mr. Hinkle would never be caught dead in an outfit like that. "But if we could just talk to him—"

"He isn't here," Mr. Long Legs said.

Miguel began to edge away, Abe with him. Abe was hanging his head as if he'd just asked for a whole rack of merchandise in Hinkle's and was being scolded for it.

But Fawn was practically digging her heels into the sidewalk. Will took a step and got between her and Long Legs.

"Do you know if you have any waste paper you want to donate?" he said. "It's for the war."

He half-expected Long Legs to chase them all off, but to his surprise, he threw back his cue ball of a head and gave a harsh laugh.

"What's so funny?" Fawn said.

She tried to dodge her way out from behind Will, but he jockeyed around to keep himself between them.

"Did I say something wrong?" Will said.

"No," Long Legs said. "You said something stupid! Do you know how sick I am—how sick *everybody* is—of giving and giving and giving to a 'war effort' that hasn't done a thing to end the war?" He opened his hand and began to tick things off on his long, bony fingers. "They've rationed our food. They won't make us new tires. They've slapped us with a 2 percent sales tax. And now we have this ridiculous dimout—" He stabbed a finger in the air in the direction of Hinkle's sign. "Neon signs are banned. We have to close the store at dusk. We have a midnight curfew." He gave the harsh-sounding laugh again. "You really think worrying about a paper shortage is going to end the war? That does about as much good as living on beans the way we're doing. And after three and a half years, most of us don't even know what the stupid war's about anyway."

"Have you forgotten Pearl Harbor?" Will said. His blood was surging, but somehow it felt good. He hadn't had a decent argument with anybody in a while.

"Pearl Harbor," the man said, looking as if he wanted to spit. "All that did was make everybody stand up and sing 'The Star-Spangled Banner.' It brought us all together, but we didn't know where we were supposed to go from there. We don't know where the blame war is supposed to be taking us."

"They talk about it on the radio all the time!" Will said. "They're tryin' to save democracy so the world won't be taken over by somebody like Hitler or the Japanese."

"Right, kid," Long Legs said. "World War I was supposed to do that back in '17. Here it is 1945 and we're still fighting about the same things! Bring our boys home; let those people over there in Europe fight their own battles."

"You wouldn't say that if the battles were bein' fought here, in America!" Will said. "If your mother and father were missing in Germany like his—" Will jerked his head toward Abe, who was now whimpering and trying to make himself invisible behind Miguel.

"And you're going to rescue them with your little red wagon?" Long Legs said. He poked a finger toward Will, as if he were ready to debate. But then he let the finger drop and grunted. "Why am I wasting my time standing around arguing with a kid?" He jerked his head toward the sidewalk. "Go on, scram, all of you. We're trying to run a business here."

Abe leapt out from behind Miguel as if he'd just been waiting for an invitation to exit, and Miguel himself took a few steps sideways, toward Guarantee Shoes.

I guess we might as well leave, Will thought, though his own next argument was pushing to be let out.

He nodded to Fawn and was about to start down the sidewalk himself when Long Legs said, "If the war drags on much longer, I say we just let Hitler and the Japs take us over. We're living like prisoners of war anyway."

Will could feel himself stiffening. His skin prickled as if he'd just collided with a cactus.

"Hey, listen, mister," he said. "You don't know what you're talkin' about! Fellas are dyin' in prisoner-of-war camps—"

The rest of it faded on Will's lips as he watched the man's eyes suddenly spring open as if he were seeing a bullet coming toward him. He was. Fawn had dropped the wagon handle and was hurling herself straight into his chest.

✝︎·✝︎·✝︎

Chapter Two

T he wagon turned on its side and dumped its load of waste
paper on the sidewalk, where the breeze picked it up and
swirled it around like big confetti.

One piece caught the long-legged man square in the face, the
wind plastering it onto his nose.

"Blast you rotten brats!" Long Legs shouted. He swatted the
paper away with one hand and tried to swat Fawn off with the
other, but she had him in a vice with her legs and was pelting
his striped shoulders with both fists.

Will knew it was going to take more than a swat or two to
peel Fawn off before she blacked the guy's eye.

I don't really care if she does, personally, he thought. *But
she's gonna get in so much trouble with Mom if I don't stop her.*

Will looked at Abe, who was still half-hiding behind Miguel—
or at least trying to. Both of them were looking at Will, obviously
waiting for instructions.

"Get her off, Abe," Will said. He had to yell to be heard over
Fawn's hollering and the man's shouting.

Abe's hazel eyes grew to the size of bicycle tires, and he shook his head.

"Ya gotta!" Will said. "Before he hurts her!"

There wasn't much chance of that, but the idea was enough to get Abe moving. Although he was ducking his head as if he were avoiding flying bullets, he dove into the fray and came out holding Fawn at arm's length under both of her armpits. Will had to dodge her feet, which kicked angrily as Abe blinked at him, his face a question mark.

"Don't let go of her 'til I say!" Will shouted. "Come on!" And he took off running. He could hear Abe's heavy footfalls right behind him—and Fawn's shrieks of "Let me go, you big oaf, or so help me I'll clobber you!"

Will glanced over his shoulder as he tore down the sidewalk toward San Francisco Street. Miguel was just tossing the last of the paper into the wagon, while Long Legs stood over him, screaming until his face turned purple.

"Forget the papers!" Will called out to him. "Come on!"

But Miguel grabbed the wagon handle before he took off. Mr. Long Legs didn't follow, but he did continue to holler like he'd been robbed blind until long after Will and his parade rounded the corner.

Fawn, too, kept screeching until they got all the way to St. Francis Cathedral, where Will stopped to let Miguel catch up to them.

"Make him put me down!" Fawn cried.

Abe shook his head, his eyes wild with fright.

"Do you promise not to beat up on Abe?" Will said.

"Yes!" Fawn said. " 'Cause I'm gonna beat up on *you!*"

"Keep holding her, Abe," Will said.

"Okay—okay! I won't hit you!" Fawn said. "Just make him let me go!"

Will nodded at Abe, who dropped Fawn into the dust without

ceremony and once more jumped behind Miguel, who had by now arrived with a wagon only one-quarter filled. The rest of its contents, Will knew, were now strewn all over the Plaza.

Fawn scowled at Abe as she picked herself up and smacked the dirt off of her rolled-up dungarees. Miguel, too, was rolling his up, to reveal a raw-looking scrape on each knee.

"What happened?" Will said.

"It was nothing," Miguel said. "I fell."

"Well, you got 'nothing' on your elbows, too," Fawn said, pointing. "Jeepers—you're bleeding!"

Abe gave a gasp and put his fist on his mouth. Will knew he'd be whimpering any minute. He didn't like it when anybody in their little group got hurt.

"It'll be okay, soon as you get it cleaned up," Will said quickly. "Let's go to your house. Your mom can bandage you up."

"She is not at home," Miguel said. "She has gone to the ranch."

"What ranch?" Fawn said.

"So we'll go to *my* house," Will said.

"My house, too!" Abe said.

"Not really, Abe," Will told him. "You're just staying there right now while Reverend Bud and Tina are away—"

"What ranch?" Fawn said.

"Your mother will not mind?" Miguel said.

"Nah. She's—"

"What ranch?"

Fawn's nostrils were flaring, a sure sign she was about to hurl herself at somebody again.

Will looked at Miguel. "I think you better tell us."

Miguel nodded, but he glanced down at his bloody knees.

"Hey, Abe," Will said. "Carry Miguel, would you?"

Abe scooped Miguel up into his big arms and mumbled

happily as he headed down Cathedral Place. Fawn was right on his heels.

"*Now* tell us about the ranch," she said.

Miguel looked over Abe's shoulder at Fawn and Will as they walked.

"We have sold our farm in Chimayo," he said. "But the new owners did not want our horses."

"You had horses?" Fawn said.

"Of course they did," Will said. "How are you gonna run a farm without horses?"

"Uncle José brought them here," Miguel went on, "but we had no place to keep them."

"You could keep 'em at Mama Hutchie's!" Fawn said. "She wouldn't mind!"

Will rolled his eyes. "Where are we gonna put them, Fawn? They aren't sleeping with ME."

"We have a place," Miguel said. "They will stay at Señor Tarantino's ranch. I mean—*Mr.* Tarantino."

"*Our* Mr. Tarantino?" Will said. "The principal?"

Miguel nodded and smiled.

Will had to smile too. If it had been any other principal, he wouldn't have been grinning. But the principal at Harrington Junior High, "Mr. T." as they called him, was a different story. Will suddenly had visions of visiting Miguel's horses *and* getting to hang around with Mr. T. at the same time. It was one of the happier thoughts he'd had lately.

"My mother is there," Miguel said. "She must go every day to take care of the horses."

How can Señora Otero get enough gas to drive out to Mr. T.'s ranch way south of town with gas still being rationed? Will thought.

Will's mother, he knew, would say he worried far too much for a 12 year old. But he didn't feel like a kid anymore. The war had made him feel like a grown-up man who didn't even have to shave yet.

He didn't have a chance to ask though, because with Canyon Road in sight, Abe had picked up the pace, and Will and Fawn were having to run to keep up. Abe always got excited when the Hutchinson house was close by. He was only staying with Will, Fawn, and Will's mother Ingrid while Abe's foster parents were in Washington, D.C., trying to make his adoption final, but Abe considered it "his house," and he loved being there.

"Wait up!" Will said.

But Abe only picked up the pace, crossing the Castillo Bridge on Paseo de Peralta at a trot. Just to the left was Canyon Road, where Abe broke into a dead run. Miguel held on with both hands, and his head bobbed as if it were on a spring. Dust flew out from Abe's feet as he flew between the brown earthen buildings that lined the dirt road, and the lilacs winding around the rail fences were startled by the flap of his jacket.

By the time they got to Will's house, Will was out of breath. He was glad his mom was in the backyard and not upstairs. He wasn't sure he would have made it that far.

Ingrid Hutchinson's blondish, streaked-with-gray hair shone in the New Mexico sun as she bent over the victory garden. All through the war she had planted a garden in the spring so that she and the kids could eat their own vegetables and let those from the big American farms go to soldiers overseas.

She looked up as the motley crew crossed the yard, shading her eyes with one hand and pushing wisps of hair back with the other. Will knew it was the sight of Abe carrying a bloodied Miguel that got her springing to her feet.

"What on earth has happened now?" she said. She wiped her hands on the back of her dress as she hurried toward them.

"He fell," Will said.

"I can see that. Let me have a look, Miguel."

"He was running from a moron!" Fawn said.

"Fawn," Mom said, her eyes studying the scrapes on Miguel's knees. "You know I don't allow tearing-down talk. Only building-up."

"*He* wasn't building up, Mama Hutchie!" Fawn said. "He said we oughta just let the Japanese and the Germans take over! He said bad stuff about the prisoners of war!"

Mom looked quickly at Will.

"It's true," Will said. "We were just asking him for waste paper and he told us we were wasting our time supporting the war effort."

"That is not true, is it, Señora Hutchinson?"

Mom looked at Miguel, and at Fawn and Will and Abe. Then she pressed her lips together before she said, "Everybody in the kitchen. Will, get the first-aid kit. Fawn, pour everybody a glass of milk. There is *stollen* in the cupboard."

"Goodies?" Fawn said.

She's already forgotten about the moron, Will thought. That happened when sweets appeared unexpectedly, since sugar was rationed as if it were gold.

When they were all settled in the kitchen—Mom doctoring Miguel's knees and elbows and the kids dipping their *stollen* in milk—Mom's face grew serious. She didn't twitch her lips the way she usually did when she talked to the kids, as if she were always on the brink of a smile. She was grim.

"This man who told you your efforts are a waste of time—" she said.

"Moron," Fawn muttered.

"He is *wrong*. The Allies are winning the war. We hear it on the radio every single day. As soon as the Axis powers surren-der—and they *will*—it will all be over. But until then, we owe it to all the men over there to do everything we can over *here* to provide what they need." She looked hard at each one of them. "Do you understand?"

They all nodded. Abe, Miguel, and Fawn looked reassured. Will tried to feel that way, but it was hard. Maybe Mom was right. Maybe he did worry too much.

"Take a couple of aspirin, Miguel," Mom said. She dug into the first-aid kit and produced a small square tin which she popped open with her fingers. "And then smile—all of you— because I have a surprise for you."

"Surprise!" Abe crowed. His grin was so wide, it was as if the word alone was enough.

"What is it?" Fawn said.

"We've been invited to Mr. Tarantino's ranch for supper," Mom said. "And since I have Reverend Bud's car while he's away, we can all go."

A cheer went up from all the kids, and Mom had to shout over it to tell them all to get cleaned up. While Miguel stayed in the kitchen with Mom so she could finish doctoring him up, Will and Abe took the steps up to Will's room two at a time. Will rummaged through his drawers for a clean polo shirt. Abe bounded onto Will's bed and studied the map on the wall.

It was a map of the islands in the Pacific where part of the war was being fought. Will's Uncle Al, who was in an intelligence unit, had given Will some tiny magnetic airplanes, which he used to mark the islands the Allies had taken from the Japanese. Abe was gazing at them now, and just as Will knew he would, he said, "Tell about war, Will."

Will sighed. "I told you the whole thing already this morning, pal."

"Tell," Abe said.

Will worked on unbuttoning his shirt as he pointed to the map. "See that little island right up there? That's Iwo Jima. Our guys started at Guadalcanal—right there—back at the beginning of the war, and they've knocked out the Japanese in the Gilbert Islands, the Marshall Islands, and the Mariana Islands." He dropped his shirt on the floor and poked a finger at the last of a necklace of islands on the map. "When we're done with Iwo Jima and we take Okinawa, then all that's left is Japan itself. We're not gonna quit until Japan surrenders unconditionally."

He said the last word—*unconditionally*—very slowly for Abe, who watched Will's lips move as he moved his own to repeat it.

"Y'know what that means?" Will asked.

Abe shook his head.

"That means they have to give up and say they've lost and then turn all the decisions about their future over to the Allies— that's us and our friends. And not just Japan but Germany and Italy, too."

He yanked the clean polo shirt over his head and watched Abe. No matter how many times Will told him about the war, he was never sure Abe really understood. Even though his own parents were still missing in Germany, where they had gone to try to help their Jewish relatives escape from Hitler when Abe was just a baby, he seemed content with his new family, Reverend Bud and Tina, and his friends. It was as if, to him, the war that was going on all over the world was just a story he liked to hear about.

"Kamikaze!" Abe said suddenly. "Tell about kamikaze!"

Will picked up his comb from the dresser and tried to plaster down his cowlick. "Kamikaze means 'divine wind' in Japanese," he said. "It's named for the typhoon that came up a long time ago and saved Japan from an invasion by this bad guy, Kublai Khan. The Japanese said the sun goddess sent the divine wind and saved 'em. So now, the pilots that go on suicide missions in planes call themselves kamikazes."

Will stopped and looked at the map of the ocean where, he had read in *TIME* magazine, ships were being bombarded by kamikazes every day—pilots who flew with their bombs and plunged both themselves and their bombs into their targets to make sure they got there. So far, the Japanese had sunk 17 ships and damaged 90 others. It wasn't the part he liked to talk about.

But as he told Abe about it for the hundredth time, a thought came to him that he *did* like.

If the guys over there have to put up with that and they're *not giving up,* he told himself, *then* I'm *not giving up, either.*

"Rudy," Abe said.

Will looked at him sharply. He was pointing to Bataan, where Will's father, Rudy Hutchinson, had been captured with the rest of the 200th Coast Artillery. As best as anyone could tell them, he was a prisoner of war there and had been for three years. Whenever Will doubted it, all he had to do was look in the scrapbook under his bed, where he had saved every clipping from the *Santa Fe New Mexican* about the 200th.

"That's where he is, all right," Will said to Abe. "But he's gonna get out, 'cause our guys are gonna get him out. And if they can do that, then we have to keep supporting them over here. We *have* to!"

Abe whimpered faintly and stuck his fist in his mouth. Will looked down to see that his own fists were doubled at his sides. He knew his face was probably bright red.

"Mad?" Abe said.

"Yeah," Will said. "But I'm not mad at you, pal. I'm just mad."

And he stayed that way as he and Miguel and Fawn and Abe piled into Reverend Bud's rattletrap of a Chevrolet with Mom and rode several miles south of Santa Fe to Mr. Tarantino's ranch. Will had never been there before, and on most days he would have had his nose pressed to the window in the backseat, studying the landscape of mountains and piñon pines, hoping to see a jackrabbit or a mule deer or possibly an elk. But now all he could think about was his own anger.

How dare that Percy Pants at Hinkle's talk that way about the prisoners, he fumed. *I shoulda let Fawn clobber him.*

"Hey," Fawn said, poking him in the side. "What's eating you?"

"Nothing," Will said. And yet he thought, *Everything.*

His mood lightened a little when they arrived at Mr. T.'s ranch—only because it was hard to stay worked up when Mr. T. was around.

The tall, white-haired principal strode out of the long, low, Spanish-style adobe house wearing his usual boots and slim dungarees and big silver belt buckle adorned with a turquoise stone. He was grinning as he squinted at the group in the car. Mr. T. always squinted, it seemed to Will, even when it wasn't sunny outside. It was one of the things that made his brown, weathered face so pleasant.

"Bienvenido, mi amigos!" he said.

"That means 'Welcome, my friends,' " Fawn informed Will.

"I know!" Will said. "I'm not an idiot."

Will could feel his mother giving him one of her looks—the one that said *There is no need to be rude, William.*

Will didn't look back at her. It was hard not to be rude when everything was suddenly getting on his nerves.

Mr. T. was already headed for the ranch house—the *hacienda,* as the Spanish would say—with one arm around Abe and one around Miguel, and Fawn attached to his back like a hobo's bag.

"Come in, come in!" he was saying, in that voice that was so surprisingly like a professor's, coming as it did out of a cowboy's mouth. "Wait 'til you see the supper Señora Otero is cooking!"

"I thought she was here to get the horses settled," Mom said as she and Will followed the group inside.

"I roped her into cooking just this once," Mr. T. said. "An old bachelor like me never passes up a chance for a home-cooked meal."

Will knew Mr. T. wasn't really a bachelor. His wife had died some years before, his mother had told him, but it still made him too sad to talk about her, even to call himself a widower.

Will could smell Señora Otero's cooking the minute the thick carved-wood front door was open. There was goat cheese involved, he would bet his life on it. Miguel's mother could do amazing things with goat cheese and sun-dried tomatoes.

"This is absolutely beautiful," Mom was saying.

Will looked around and had to admit she was right. The house was the usual Santa Fe style with thick, cream-colored adobe walls rubbed smooth with sheepskin and rounded at the corners, and viga beams—whole logs stripped of their bark—crisscrossing the low ceilings. But it was more elegant than any home Will had ever been in here in New Mexico.

The living room was lined on one side with shelves packed with volumes that smelled of leather, and on the other side it looked out through large arched windows to a patio that was catching and holding the afternoon light on its brightly colored tiles.

As Mr. T. showed them around, Will saw spacious bedrooms with windowed doors opening into small private patios, and bathrooms with sunken tubs, and a huge open Spanish kitchen with an Indian style kiva fireplace in the corner. Mom said she could move right into the sun room and read books all day sprawled out on the Navajo rug. Fawn said her personal favorite was the dining room, and Will had to agree. It looked noble with its hand-carved table and its chest full of Indian pottery pieces worn smooth with use.

Mom fingered the curtains on the small dining room window. "I wouldn't have figured you to be one for lace," she said to Mr. T., her lips twitching.

"My housekeeper," he said. "I don't know what I'm going to do without her."

"Why do you have to?" Mom said.

"I've lost her. She's moved to Albuquerque to be closer to her family."

Fawn gave Will a poke in the side. "This is getting boring," she whispered to him.

Will cleared his throat, and Mr. T. looked at him, his eyebrows up.

"Could we maybe see the horses?" Will said.

"Now, that *is* the point, isn't it?" Mr. T. said. He motioned toward the door that led out of the kitchen. "My boys ought to be taking them into the stables right about now. Go out and have a look."

He didn't have to tell them twice. Will, Miguel, and Fawn were out the back door and climbing up onto the corral fence almost before he finished the sentence. Only Abe lingered behind, and when he caught up with the others, Will saw his fist heading into his mouth.

"What's wrong, pal?" Will said.

"He looks scared," Fawn said. "Are ya scared, Abe?"

Abe nodded and pointed toward the corral. Will followed with his eyes, but all he saw were three horses moving toward them, their heads bobbing as they walked. The closer they came, the farther Abe backed away.

"You're not afraid of *them*, are you?" Will said.

Abe nodded again and added a whimper.

Will looked back at the horses. They weren't even as big as most of the quarter horses Will used to ride when he and his parents were living at the Los Alamos Ranch School. There was one Appaloosa, whose spotted markings gave him the look of a toy, and a mustang with a shaggy mane and tail that wouldn't have frightened a baby at a birthday party. The third, a muscular work horse with fly bites freckling his reddish shanks, was larger than the others, but he immediately nuzzled his nose into Miguel's palm and whinnied softly.

"They're sweet!" Fawn said as she threw her arms around the mustang's neck.

That didn't appear to be enough reassurance for Abe. He kept backing up until he ran into the adobe wall of the stable. The skull of a steer, which hung above his head for decoration, came loose from its nail and tumbled down the wall, landing right next to Abe's foot. He gave a howl and took off running for the house.

"Are we gonna get in trouble for that?" Fawn said.

"Why would we?" Will said. "It wasn't our fault."

"I will go and make sure he is all right," Miguel said.

As he disappeared into the house, Fawn climbed to a higher rail on the fence and pointed beyond the horse corral.

"Mr. T.'s got cattle, too," she said.

Will fingered the Appaloosa's mane as he looked where Fawn was pointing, to a field at the foot of a dotted hill. It was getting close to sunset, so Will could see only their silhouettes in the fading light, but there was a small herd grazing in the meager underbrush.

"Who are those guys?" Fawn said.

"What guys?"

"The ones riding their horses onto the field," Fawn said. "See?"

Will did see. There were two men on horseback riding toward the fringes of the herd. The cattle were obviously used to the presence of horsemen because they barely lifted their heads as one of the men twirled a lariat in the air and neatly dropped its lasso over one steer's head, barely touching his horns with the rope. The other man did the same to another steer, and both led the cattle away from the herd and disappeared into a stand of trees.

"They were pretty good at that," Fawn said.

Will didn't answer right away—not until he turned to Fawn with eyes he knew were wide open.

"Fawn," he said. "What if they just stole Mr. T.'s. cattle?"

✢ ⬥ ✢

Chapter Three

*L*et's go after 'em!" Fawn said.

She was already on the ground before Will was able to grab her by the arm.

"Don't be a goof!" he said. "You're gonna run after them? On foot? They have horses, for Pete's sake!"

"We gotta do *some*thing!"

"We have to tell Mr. T.," Will said. "And quick!"

They both tore across the stable yard and up the path to the back door. Fawn led the way into the kitchen, where she nearly plowed into Señora Otero and a platter of spare ribs oozing chili sauce.

"What is out there that has you children barreling in here like you've seen the burning bush?" Mom said. "First Abe, then Miguel, now you two—"

"Some men, Mr. T.!" Fawn said before Will could even get his mouth open. "They're stealing your cattle!"

Mr. T. reached over and switched Benny Goodman off the radio and grinned at Fawn.

"You have a wild imagination, young'un," he said. "Ingrid, you let her listen to entirely too many Westerns on the radio."

"It's not my imagination!" Fawn said. Her face was beet red, and Will was afraid she was going to lunge right at Mr. T. any second.

"It's not," Will said. "We saw two men on horses rope two of your steers and take them from the field." Will made an X on his chest with his finger. "I promise—it happened!"

"I'm sure it did," Mr. T. said. He folded his hands behind his white head and leaned back. "Those were my ranch hands. I just bought a few more steers when I moved down here, and they probably haven't been branded yet. I can't afford that much help around here, so those boys work some long hours."

"Why *did* you move down here?" Mom asked.

"Government needed that land north of town where I had my last ranch. This one's smaller, but it's still enough to support me, along with my school salary, of course, and to let me contribute to the war effort—"

"They sure acted suspicious for ranch hands," Will said. "Why would they take 'em into the trees? Why wouldn't they just bring them to the barn?"

Mr. T.'s grin faded. One of the things Will liked about him was that he took kids seriously—not like some adults who got the isn't-that-cute look on their faces when they were talking to people under 18.

"I really think they were stealing," Will said. "I'm not making it up."

"He's not," Fawn said.

"I know you're not," Mr. T. said. "You're good kids—you wouldn't do that." He reached out and tugged gently at one of Fawn's braids. "But cattle thieving only happens in the movies these days. Last time I saw it was in a John Wayne film."

"There's been a revival of cattle rustling in the last few

months!" Will said. "I read about it in the *Saturday Evening Post*. It's because of the beef shortages—"

"Will, that's enough," Mom said. Her voice was soft, but her mouth wasn't twitching.

"But it's true!" Will said.

"I'm sure it is, but there's no sense upsetting everybody."

"Supper is ready," said another, even quieter voice from the dining room doorway. It was Señora Otero, Miguel's mother, holding a plate of *posole*, the brown-crusted bread toasted with butter, garlic, and cheese that Will loved.

But suddenly he'd lost his appetite. *I'm tryin' to help here,* he thought, *and nobody's listening to me!*

It was one more thing to make his bad mood worse. If he didn't get to argue with somebody about something in the next five minutes, he was sure he was going to explode right there at the supper table.

He wanted to excuse himself and go pout by the horse corral, but he knew his mother would never go for that kind of rudeness. The closest he could come was not closing his eyes during the blessing. He stared angrily at his lap until Mr. T. led a round of amens. When he lifted his head, Señora Otero was looking at him.

Miguel's mother was a beautiful woman. Even Will, who seldom gave girls a second look, knew that. Although she wore her wavy black hair pulled straight back into a bun at the nape of her neck and didn't thin out her eyebrows the way most ladies-in-fashion did, she was stunning with her heart-shaped lips, her skin the color of coffee with cream, and her dark, liquid eyes. She was slender and delicate and wrote poetry. Will could never picture her working on a farm, even though he had seen her be strong when she had to be. He was pretty sure he would have thought she was beautiful even if she hadn't been all those things, however. They had always seemed to understand each other and be able to talk without speaking a word.

Right now, her lovely dark eyes were searching his face as if she were trying to find clues to his mood. He could feel his cheeks turning red.

"I have a favor to ask of you, Will," she said, with just a hint of a Spanish accent that curved her perfectly spoken words upward at the ends. "Of all of you children."

"Anything," Will said, and felt his skin go a deeper shade of crimson.

"Señor Tarantino has been kind enough to allow me to board my horses here, but I am unable to exercise them as they need to be now that they are no longer working horses."

"You want us to do it?" Fawn said. "Ride them every day?"

"That's no favor," Will said. "That would be too perfect!"

"Before you start signing any contracts," Mom said, "there's more to it than just going out for a ride. Right?"

Señora Otero nodded. "You would help feed them and give them hay in their stalls, water them, and sweep up after them."

"That part is icky," Miguel said. "The sweeping."

"Icky, *mi hijo?*" Señora Otero said, as if the word itself had a bad smell. Miguel squirmed in his seat.

"You characters are a bad influence on Miguel," Mom said to Will and Fawn. "He's starting to pick up your slang."

"Does that mean we can't take care of the horses?" Fawn said.

"No, no!" Señora Otero said. "You will do a fine job, I know."

"You can ride your bicycles out here after school," Mom said. "It isn't that far."

"Abe doesn't have a bike, though," Fawn said.

Will looked at Abe, who was currently stuffing his entire napkin into his mouth and looking helplessly back at him.

"He doesn't get out of school 'til almost dark," Will said. "Besides, I don't think he'll mind missing horseback riding."

Abe pulled the napkin out of his mouth and grinned widely at Will.

"Good, then," Señora Otero said. "We have an agreement."

It was enough to make Will feel a little better—and enough to help him get down several spare ribs and two helpings of *posole* and dipping sauce.

But in spite of how relieved he looked at the dinner table, it didn't make Abe feel completely better. Several times during the night as they slept in Will's upstairs room, Abe sat straight up in bed, whimpering and talking gibberish about "Horse! Big horse!" From what Will could gather, the big horses in question were chasing Abe all over New Mexico in his dreams.

"You don't have to be scared of those horses, pal," Will tried to reassure him. "In the first place, you're almost as big as they are! They could practically ride *you!*"

That didn't help. From then on, Abe's nightmares were evidently filled with images of giant Appaloosas climbing onto his back. By the time the alarm rang to get up for church, Will was crankier than ever.

And the sermon at church just made things worse.

Reverend Bud was out of town for one thing, and although he was only the associate pastor, Will liked his sermons much better than Reverend Weston's. He didn't tell good stories the way Bud did, and half the time Will's mind wandered from the big words he was using to whatever was going on outside the window. Even a passing raven was more interesting than Reverend Weston's commentaries.

Will couldn't ignore him that day, though, because the Bible text for the sermon got his blood boiling again.

"And Jesus said," Reverend Weston boomed, " 'Ye hath heard that it hath been said: An eye for an eye, and a tooth for a tooth.' "

Sounds good so far, Will thought. *That's what our guys are doing in the war.*

"And then Jesus went on to say, 'But I say unto you, That ye resist not evil: but whosoever shall smite thee on thy right cheek, turn to him the other also.'"

Will sat straight up in his seat. *Jesus said that?* he wanted to call out to Reverend Weston—except that the poor man would probably have been startled right out of the pulpit. *Jesus said we shouldn't fight back when somebody attacks us? No, Jesus was tough. He never woulda said that!*

But Reverend Weston continued, telling how Jesus said if somebody wants to sue you and take your coat, you should give him your entire wardrobe, and how if someone forces you to walk a mile with him, you should walk two.

"'But I say unto you,'" the reverend read from the big black Bible in front of him, "'Love your enemies, bless them that curse you, do good to them that hate you, and pray for them which despitefully use you, and persecute you.'"

Though Will wasn't sure what every word of that meant, he had the general idea. But it couldn't possibly be right.

Jesus wouldn't be a Percy Pants like that, he told himself. *And He wouldn't want us being all lovey-dovey about the Japanese and the Germans.*

"As the war goes on," Reverend Weston was saying, "our anger and our hate are stirred, but we must beware. The time is now to do as Jesus says and love our enemies, pray for those who hate us."

Then Jesus can forget it, Will thought stubbornly. *I wouldn't be caught dead doing that! Love those evil people who took my dad prisoner? Ha!*

The longer Reverend Weston droned on, the angrier Will got. When the sermon was finally over, it was all he could do not to burst into applause out of sheer relief, and when the final hymn faded out, Will was the first one out the heavy wooden doors. He was sitting at the bottom of the rock slab steps when Mom found him.

"Penny for your thoughts," she said as she slipped in next to him and tucked her dress around her knees.

Will just shrugged. He was afraid if he opened his mouth, something would come out that would get him restricted to his room for the rest of his life.

His mother waited. The silence, broken only by the first voices of the people coming out of the church above them, was almost worse than being restricted.

"I'm sick of everything," he said.

"Uh-huh."

"I want Dad home."

"Yeah."

"And I know I have to keep praying and all that and God'll take care of it—but I want to take care of something. I'm sick of waiting around!"

"Mmm-hmm."

"And everybody thinks I'm a kid, only I don't feel like a kid anymore and I'd rather be a kid, only I can't because the war won't let me."

"Ah."

Will looked miserably at his mother. Her lips weren't twitching. Her eyes were drooped at the corners. She understood. But she didn't say a word.

"So what do I do?" he said.

Slowly, Mom shook her head. "I have absolutely no idea, son. I have no solutions, no answers, no assurances. All I can do is try to make this as easy for you as I can."

Will clasped his hands around his shins and shrugged again. "Thanks, but there's no way you can do that."

"Oh," Mom said. "That's really too bad. I guess I'll cancel our reservation, then."

"What reservation?" Will said.

"It doesn't matter, if it isn't going to cheer you up."

Her lips *were* twitching now, and Will was curious in spite of himself.

"Maybe it could," he said. "What is it?"

"Just lunch at the Pink Adobe for you and Fawn and Abe and me."

Will let his own lips twitch. "Oh, all right," he said. "I guess I could gag something down."

"That's what I thought," Mom said.

The Pink Adobe was Will's second favorite place to eat in Santa Fe, second only to the Plaza Café. The Pink Adobe had just opened the year before, and Rosalie Murphy, the owner, served Spanish food that was almost as good as Señora Otero's. But it was really the way the place felt that made Will love to go there. It was pink on the outside, which didn't exactly thrill him. On the inside, however, was a maze of rooms, some of them dark and mysterious, others bright white with colored tiles around their kiva fireplaces. Will and Fawn were both determined to eat in every one of the rooms before the end of 1945, and that Sunday Rosalie Murphy gladly led them to a cheery room they hadn't dined in before, with white stucco walls and lace curtains at the arched windows that made sunny patterns on the tablecloths.

"It looks like I'm going to have to get lace curtains," Mom said as they sat down at their tile-topped table. "Everyone else has them."

Will ignored the curtains and studied the menu. He had just decided on the paella when Fawn poked him.

"What?" Will said, rubbing his ribs.

"Look at those men over there."

Her whisper carried across the table, so Mom, too, looked in the direction Fawn was jerking her head.

"Are you talking about the men with the beards?" Mom said.

Fawn nodded. Just a table away from them there were four men ordering lunch, and each one of them had a fully hairy chin. It was an unusual thing to see in Santa Fe, since most of the residents were Mexican or Indian—not men known for bearded faces. Very few of the Anglos went in for beards. It was the style for men to be clean-shaven. In fact, the only bearded men Will had ever seen were in pictures of his Hutchinson ancestors.

"Who are they?" Will said.

"Why are they all hairy?" Fawn asked.

Mom shrugged. "Do you think we should ask them?"

"No," Will said. "Wouldn't that be rude? 'Hey, mister. How come you don't shave?' "

"I'll ask them," Fawn said, already scraping her chair back noisily on the glazed-tile floor.

"Don't ask them like *that*," Mom said. "Just politely inquire."

"Huh?" Fawn said.

Abe looked over the top of his menu and also said, "Huh?" though Will was sure he had no idea what was going on.

"I'll ask them," Mom said.

But before she could get up, one of the men, the one with the reddest, bushiest beard, looked up at her and smiled.

"You want to know about our beards?" he said.

"As a matter of fact, yes!" Mom said.

"Can't you afford razors?" Fawn said.

This time, Will poked *her*.

"We can afford them, little missy," Red Beard said. "We've just made a pledge not to shave until the war is completely over."

Fawn let out a long whistle. Mom frowned and said, "Not in a restaurant, Fawn."

"But for real, mister?" Fawn said. "Even if it takes months and months—even years?"

"It's not gonna take that long!" Will said. He could feel his blood going hot again. "We're gonna wipe up the floor with those Axis powers in—six months, I bet! Maybe less!"

"I hope so," said the man with the gray beard that had grown in thin and straggly. "This thing is really starting to itch."

"Then prepare to scratch, my friend," said still another voice. "Because this war isn't going to be over for a long, long time."

Hot words were already on Will's lips before he turned around to see who was spouting such baloney. When his eyes lit on the man, they began to smolder.

It was Long Legs.

✝ ✦ ✝

Chapter Four

*U*h-oh," Fawn said under her breath. She picked up her menu and hid behind it.

Abe whimpered and tried to get under the table. When that proved unsuccessful, he put his menu on top of his head and whimpered some more.

Will, meanwhile, was hurling daggers at Long Legs with his eyes. The tall man, dressed today in a suit with shoulder pads the size of pillows, seemed to feel Will's glare and turned to see who was stabbing him.

"Well, well, well," he said as his eyes flickered with recognition. "The young fanatic—and his evil little friend."

He had by now spotted Fawn peering out from behind her menu. Once she knew he'd seen her, she dropped it and scowled at him until Will was sure her eyebrows would reach her chin.

"Is there a little history I should know about here?" Mom said, looking from Long Legs to Fawn to Will and back again.

"Are these your brats, lady?" Long Legs said.

Will watched his mother stiffen. "I am responsible for all of these *children,* if that's what you mean," she said. There wasn't a twitch in sight.

"Then tell 'em not to come around Hinkle's asking for handouts anymore. We're trying to run a business, and the war's making it hard enough as it is without a bunch of kids coming in with their speeches about how we have to keep supporting the war effort."

"I see," Mom said. "That's quite enough information, thank you."

Long Legs seemed reluctant to let it go at that, but Mom was clearly telling him with her eyes to get lost. Will didn't want him to "get lost" yet—not until he'd had a chance to tell *his* side of the story.

"Mom, that's not how it was at all," Will said.

"Fine," Mom said. "But I'm sure this gentleman has other business to attend to."

"Gentleman?" Fawn muttered.

"But Mom—" Will said.

"Enough. And you, sir," Mom turned to Long Legs. "We'd like to get on with our lunch now if you don't mind."

"Sure," Long Legs said. "But you just make sure you tell them—"

"I will."

"You don't have to tell us, Mom!" Will said. "I wouldn't go back to his old store if my life depended—"

"Will, enough," Mom said.

Long Legs edged away and then hurried off to another room in the Pink Adobe, as if he were afraid Mom's stern tone was going to be directed at him next. Will stared at her.

"Are you taking his side?" he said.

"Of course not," Mom said. "But there was no point in discussing it further. Some ditches are not worth dying in."

"What's that mean?" Fawn asked.

Will ignored the explanation. He already knew what it meant, and it made him angrier than ever. *Just once,* he thought, *just once I'd like to be able to give somebody a piece of my mind.*

"I have to go to the bathroom," Fawn said.

"Go ahead," Mom said, "and show Abe where the men's room is."

"No have to," Abe said, shaking his head.

"Yes, you do," Mom said. "Go."

It didn't take a scientist to figure out that Mom was just trying to clear the room so she could give Will a talking-to. Will slumped down in his chair and scowled at the table.

"Am I to assume you didn't listen to the sermon in church today?" Mom said when Fawn and Abe were gone.

"I heard it," Will said.

"You *heard* it, but did you listen?"

"It was about Jesus being yellow."

"Excuse me?"

Mom was by now leaning across the table, which wasn't a good sign. Will slowly sat up and changed his tone.

"It was about when somebody hits you, you don't hit 'em back," Will said between tightened teeth. "You turn the other cheek so they can hit you again. I don't get that." He tried to shrug off his anger, but it stuck to him like a mass of sticky cobwebs. "We're not supposed to fight back?"

Mom sighed. "It's complicated, Son," she said. "I can try to explain it to you if you want."

She looked at him, her green eyes waiting for his answer.

I wish somebody would *explain it!* Will wanted to say. *But I don't think anybody can!*

He was, in fact, about to come out with those very words when he felt a warm hand on his shoulder. He turned to see Mr. T. smiling down at him.

"I hope I'm not interrupting," he said.

"You are," Mom said, "but I think Will is probably rather grateful to you. Join us."

She patted the empty chair, and Mr. T. folded his long self into it.

"Do you need a menu?" Mom said. "We haven't ordered yet. It seems we weren't meant to today."

Mr. T. shook his head. "No, I just tracked you down here because I have some interesting news for you."

"What?" Fawn said, skipping up to the table with a lumbering Abe behind her.

"I noticed you weren't in church this morning," Mom said. "Is everything all right?"

"Not exactly." Mr. T. looked at Will. "I kept waking up during the night last night, thinking about what you said about cattle rustling. So I got up early this morning and asked my ranch hands if they took any cattle out of the herd late yesterday. They said they never left the stable area last night."

"So those *were* thieves we saw!" Fawn cried, ignoring the finger Mom put up to her lips.

"I don't know that for sure," Mr. T. said, "but we did take stock of the herd—which was why I didn't make it to the service. If I'm not mistaken, I've got several head missing."

"And you want us to find 'em for you!" Fawn said.

She was already halfway out of her chair and probably would have bolted out the door if Mom hadn't put her hand on top of her head and pushed her back down into her seat.

Mr. T. smothered a smile and turned to Will. "So then I went and looked up that article in the *Saturday Evening Post* you were talking about. You were right. Cattle rustling has reappeared out here in the West. Couple of men have been wounded in shootouts when ranchers met up with the rustlers."

Abe's eyes grew to the size of his plate, and Fawn's weren't much smaller.

"Are you going after them with a gun?" she said.

"Fawn!" Mom said.

Mr. T. grinned, his smile white against his tanned face. "No, darlin'," he said. "They're only cattle, after all."

"But they're part of your livelihood," Mom said. "You'll do *something*, won't you?"

"Can we help?" Fawn said. "We'll help, won't we, Will?"

Will looked at his mother, whose eyebrows had shot up to her hairline.

"You can help me in one way," Mr. T. said. "Tell me everything you can remember about the men you saw."

Fawn opened her mouth, but Will clapped his hand over it. It was clearly the only way to get a word in edgewise.

"We couldn't see their faces," Will said. "It was almost dark so all we could see was their outlines."

"How many were there?"

Fawn held up two fingers as she squirmed to pull away from Will.

"Two," Will said, "and they were on horses. They each roped a steer and took it off into the trees."

"You may have caught the tail end of that caper," Mr. T. said, "because I think I have about six missing."

Fawn chomped down on Will's hand, and with a yelp he let her go. Abe yelped, too, as if it just seemed like the right thing to do just then.

"Who could hide six cattle?" Fawn said. "We could go out on the horses and find 'em for ya!"

"I don't know about this horseback riding, now that we know there are thieves around," Mom said.

Will himself almost yelped at that.

"They're out to steal cattle, Mom!" he said. "Not kids!"

Mom's lips twitched. "Not normal kids, maybe. But my brood, who always have their noses stuck in things that don't concern them, are prime targets."

"Mo-om!" Will said.

"You mean we can't ride the horses now?" Fawn said.

"Did I say that?" Mom said. She looked helplessly at Mr. T., who put his hand up before Will and Fawn could catch their breath for another wail.

"I think it will be fine for them to ride, Ingrid," he said. "As long as they promise not to go out playing Lone Ranger and Tonto." He looked sternly at Fawn and Will, though Will saw the twinkle in his eyes.

"I promise," Will said.

"But—" Fawn started to say.

When Will kicked her under the table, she stopped and just nodded.

"Good, then," Mr. T. said.

"Wait," Mom said. "I want to hear Fawn say the words. A nod is open to too much interpretation."

"What's that mean?" Fawn said.

"It means you have to *say* you promise," Will said.

He nudged her leg with his foot, threatening another kick.

"Okay," Fawn said. "I promise."

"Then I think there is no time like the present to start." Mr. T. unfolded his long legs from the chair and stood up. He was so tall, his turquoise-studded belt buckle was at Will's nose level. "Ingrid, why don't you bring them out this afternoon for their first riding lesson?"

A cheer went up from the table that even Abe participated in—although when they reached the ranch that afternoon, Abe draped himself over the corral fence and watched while Fawn, Will, and Miguel, who they picked up on the way, all climbed onto horses and began a slow walk around the corral.

All three of them had been on horseback before. Riding had been an everyday thing at the Los Alamos Ranch School, and even though Will hadn't been a student there because he was still too young, he had joined right in with his dad and the older boys. The minute he mounted Señora Otero's Cisco, the big fly-bitten workhorse, the smell of the leather and the sound of its creaking as Will settled himself onto it brought on thoughts of his father so vivid he wanted to reach out and touch him.

"You okay, fella?" said the ranch hand who was checking the children out on their riding basics. He was a tall string bean of a man with big ears and even bigger lips. His eyes were kind, and Will liked his name: Gabby.

"Yeah," Will said.

"Don't let Cisco scare you," Gabby said. "He's big, but you can outsmart him."

"I'm not scared of him," Will said. What he was scared of was not being able to get through this ride without crying for his dad. He tried to concentrate on what everyone else was doing.

Miguel was astride Hilachas, the scruffy-looking mustang. Miguel had told Will *hilachas* meant "nothing but rags." It made Will feel kind of sorry for the mangy old steed, but Miguel seemed to love him. He was leaning forward in the saddle, his face buried in Hilachas's straggly mane.

Fawn's horse was the Appaloosa, Virguela, which even Will knew was the Spanish word for chicken pox. Like all Appaloosas, Virguela was spotted, but Will thought it was kind of a cruel name. He made it a point to call her Virgy.

Both Fawn and Miguel rode well because they'd grown up on the backs of horses. Will was a little rusty, but after a few turns around the corral, he felt at home in the saddle again. He was starting to get bored, in fact, when Mr. T. strode out of the stables and hooked a foot up onto the fence rail beside Abe.

"What do you think?" Mr. T. said. "Are they ready to venture out of the corral?"

Abe nodded happily, as if he knew exactly what a word like

"venture" could possibly mean. Will suspected he was just happy that *he* didn't have to ride a horse. That was probably the only reason he was standing this close to them.

"All right, then, my young friends," Mr. T. said. "Don't go too far. We want you back before dark."

"What about Abe?" Will said.

Mr. T. slung an arm around Abe's big shoulders. "He'll keep me company, I'm sure."

"As long as you have food," Fawn said. She reined Virgy in next to the fence. The horse tossed her head and muttered under her breath.

I feel that way around Fawn sometimes too, Will thought, smiling to himself. He was already starting to feel better, just at the thought of being free to get away and clear the cobwebs out of his head. He didn't remember riding horses being good for him that way before. Of course, before, he didn't have the cobwebs of anger and war in his head, in the first place.

"You mean we can leave the ranch?" Fawn was saying. "And go anywhere we want?"

"I wouldn't want you riding all the way to Albuquerque," Mr. T. said with a chuckle. "I trust you to use good judgment."

"We will do that, señor," Miguel said.

"I know you will or I wouldn't be letting you out of my sight." Mr. T. nodded toward the stable. "Just don't forget that when you get back you'll have to feed and water the animals and clean their stalls."

Will heard that, but he wasn't sure Fawn did. Gabby was opening the gate, and Fawn was already halfway through it, Virgy kicking up dust with her hooves.

Mr. T. grinned at Will. "Try to keep her under control, would you?"

"Who?" Will said. "The horse, or Fawn?"

Mr. T. gave Cisco a slap on the shank and Will was suddenly

off, out of the corral and trotting behind Fawn, with Miguel bringing up the rear on Hilachas. They were barely out of earshot of the stables before Will began to feel something he hadn't felt in a long time. He wasn't sure what it was, but it whipped through him the same way the March air was swirling around him, and it made him notice things like the woolly patches of buffalo grass and rabbit brush, the faint scent of newly blossoming cactus flowers, the taste of the red dirt as it puffed up to his lips from the trail.

"Yeeee-haw!" he heard himself yell.

Fawn looked over her shoulder and grinned, and then let out some kind of Indian whoop that echoed up to the cliffs and back. Behind him, soft-spoken Miguel cried, *"Arriba! Arriba!"*

"What does that mean?" Fawn said.

"I don't know," Will said, "but I like it!"

So they all shouted *"Arriba! Arriba!"* as they rode across the red, gravelly dirt, amid the clumps of sagebrush and weeds, weaving in and out of the piñons and junipers and candle-shaped yucca plants. The greens of the thick, squatty trees had never seemed so crisp to Will, nor those of the chamisa plants so soft and new.

The ravens complained from the cliffs that the kids were making too much noise, and the occasional whiptail lizard skittered across their path, startled by their intrusion. Will saw and heard it all, but it didn't stop him. It was so good to be out—riding fast, yelling his head off—he felt almost wild.

"There is a stream!" Miguel called out to him at one point. "We must stop and let the horses drink!"

After all that yelling, Will thought he could use a drink himself. He and Fawn followed Miguel to an unexpected little stream that was guttering its way through the desert, the result of the melting snow in the mountains. Will climbed down from Cisco and flopped on his belly onto the ground beside his hooves to scoop water into his own mouth while Cisco lapped delicately with his velvet tongue.

"Cisco is a gentleman," Miguel said. "See how he drinks."

"I don't want him to be a gentleman," Will said. "I want him to be tough. I want him to be a fighter who doesn't take stuff from anybody."

"Stuff?" Miguel said.

"He means like nobody can give him the business," Fawn said.

Miguel smiled shyly. "I do not know 'give him the business' either," he said.

"You don't get out that much, do ya?" Fawn said.

"It means nobody can work you over—you know, really get you down," Will said.

Miguel nodded, but Will still wasn't sure he understood.

"It would be like me challenging you to a race and not letting you beat me," Will said. "Or not letting you win an argument or tease me without me clobbering you."

Miguel looked a little alarmed.

"I would never give *you* the business, Miguel," Will said quickly. "But lately, I'd sure like to give it to *some*body."

He rolled over on his back. Above him, the sky was water-colored in thin clouds, already pinking up with the start of sunset. He'd been as peaceful as the sky a few minutes ago, and now he was all worked up again. The blood was surging up into his face and burning his cheeks, and for no reason he could think of, except that he was suddenly angry.

He sat up with a jolt. "We have to get back," he said. "Let's race."

"These are not racing horses," Miguel said. "And the desert is not a safe place for—"

"So it'll be a slow race," Will said. "But the last one back has to clean *all* the stalls."

"What about the second one back?" Fawn said. She was already remounting Virgy, and a fire was igniting in her eyes.

"Second one back has to haul all the hay," Will said. "Winner just feeds and that's all."

"A slow race. You promise?" Miguel said.

"Cross my heart and hope to spit!" Will said. He swung his leg over Cisco's back and dug his heels in. "But that just depends on what you mean by 'slow'!"

One more dig, and he and Cisco were off across the desert floor, dirt spewing up behind them, pines and junipers whipping past in a blur.

Will could hear the thunder of hooves behind him, sounding for all the world like a Henry Fonda movie. He felt himself smiling again as he urged Cisco on, toward a bend in the path ahead.

"Come on, slowpokes!" he shouted over his shoulder. "Or you'll be mucking out stalls all night! *Arriba! Arri*—"

But the word—whatever it meant—died on the air as Cisco rounded the bend. Will pulled hard on the reins and leaned back in the saddle until his back almost touched the horse's.

"Whoa, Cisco!" he shouted. "Whoa!"

For there in front of him, running across the trail, was a person—a person who any second was going to be tangled up in Cisco's hooves.

☂ ⸱☂⸱ ☂

Chapter Five

L ook out!" Will shouted.

He pulled back on Cisco's reins until they were nearly under his chin, and the big horse reared up on his hind legs. Will could feel himself sliding from the saddle, and he hung on until Cisco dropped down on all fours again, jarring Will so hard his teeth knocked together. Below him, a figure with a mass of dark hair was just picking itself up from the ground.

"Are you all right?" Will said. "I'm really sorry—"

"You should be!" said a voice from under the hair. The speaker tossed the mane back and revealed a square, feminine face and a pair of indignant brown eyes. "Where did you learn to ride a horse?" she said. "No, where did you learn your manners? No—forget that—you don't *have* any manners!"

Will didn't know which question to answer first, so he just shook his head and said, "Sorry. I didn't see you—"

"Of course you didn't see me! You barreled around that curve so fast you couldn't have seen a freight train in time to stop!"

By now, Miguel and Fawn had reached them in a swirl of

dust, and Will's temper was burning in his cheeks again.

"Well, who knew there would be somebody sitting down in the middle of the road?" he said.

The girl looked around her and raised her black eyebrows at Will. "What road?" she said. "This is barely a path!"

"So?" Will said. "It isn't a park bench, so what were you doing sitting on it?"

"For your information, I was running to get out of *your* way because I heard your little stampede coming and I tripped." She pulled one leg of her dungarees up to her knee, exposing a bloody scrape. "And now I have an abrasion, thank you very much."

"What's an abrasion?" Fawn said.

The girl seemed to notice for the first time that there was someone there besides Will. Her eyes darted among the three of them, and a little of the bravado in her square chin seemed to fade.

"Just watch where you're going from now on," she said abruptly. And then she was suddenly gone, disappearing among the junipers and vanishing down a hill.

"Who was *that?*" Fawn said.

"How should I know?" Will replied.

Fawn turned from watching the girl's dust die down to studying Will's face. "What's wrong with *you?*" she said. "All I did was ask you a question. You don't have to bite my head off."

Miguel looked puzzled.

"It's just an expression, Miguel," Will said, "and I didn't bite your head off, Fawn. She just made me mad, that's all."

"Me, too," Fawn said. "I didn't like her. She used big words— like she was trying to impress us."

"Maybe she is merely smart," Miguel said.

She'd been smart all right, Will thought. Too smart. She'd

made him feel like a moron. But she'd seemed tough, too—maybe even tougher than Fawn.

"She is Spanish," Miguel said.

"She isn't nice like you and your mom, though," Fawn said.

That's because she doesn't come from up in the hills like them, Will thought. But he didn't say it. Señora Otero, his mother had told him, was a self-educated woman, but most of the people from places like Chimayo were uneducated farmers. It had amazed Will the first time he'd realized that some of them didn't even know there was a war going on, because they didn't have radios and couldn't read newspapers and just kept on with life as it had always been.

It was obvious the girl he'd almost run over with Cisco was smart *and* educated. *And she thought she was better than me,* Will added to himself. *I'd like to find her and give her a piece of my mind!*

He picked up the reins. Cisco nickered and stamped his hooves. "Let's follow her," Will said.

"Yeah!" Fawn said, and then she wrinkled her brow at Will. "How come?"

But Miguel put up his hand. "We must return to the ranch before dark," he said. He pointed at the sky. "I think we must leave now."

"Rats," Fawn said. "This was just getting good."

"Just a little while longer," Will said.

Miguel shook his head. "It is the dimout," he said. "There will be no light for us in the stable. And Señora Hutchinson must drive us home with low headlights."

"Yeah, yeah, okay," Will said. But he looked longingly through the junipers where the girl had disappeared. It sure would have felt good to argue with her a little longer.

"Are we still racing?" Fawn said to Will.

Miguel shook his head.

"You're such an old granny sometimes, Miguel," Fawn said. She edged Virgy ahead of Cisco and looked over her shoulder with a smug smile for Will. "Dare ya," she said.

But Will's interest in the race had disappeared, and he was now mulling over who that girl was and why she had made him feel like he wanted to show her that he was as smart and as tough as she was. He never felt that way around Fawn, but as he and Cisco picked their way along the trail behind her, he decided that must be because he *knew* he would never be as quick and agile as Fawn, but that he would always be several steps ahead of her mentally.

"How old do you think she was?" he said out loud.

"Who?" Fawn said.

"The señorita?" Miguel said. "Thirteen, maybe 14."

"Yeah, older than us," Fawn said. "But not by much. I could take her on."

"You don't think she could beat you?" Will said. "She wasn't as skinny as you, and I think she was taller."

"I am *not* skinny!" Fawn said.

"Yeah, you are. You're a rail. She had a little meat on her bones."

"Take that back, Will Hutchinson!" Fawn said.

Will was surprised to see her black eyes flashing at him.

"What?" he said. "What did I say?"

"Stop," Miguel said behind them.

Will reined Cisco in and looked back at Miguel, who was pointing up ahead.

"Which way is ours?" he said.

Will looked at the fork in the trail he was pointing to. One led uphill and curved off into the darkness. The other one led down and had fewer trees to make shadows.

"I don't know," Will said. "I lost track. Which way, Fawn?"

Fawn shrugged.

"You're the Indian!" Will said. "I thought you never got lost!"

"I guess I'm just not smart enough," she said. "You'd better find your smart girlfriend and ask her."

"Girlfriend?" Will said. He could feel his lip curling up. "She's not my girlfriend. I didn't even like her. I don't even know her. I don't even like girls!"

"Thank you very much," Fawn said.

"Oh, cut it out," Will said. "You're not a girl, you're—"

"Will," Miguel whispered, "if I were you, I would stop this conversation."

Will rolled his eyes and peered through the gathering dusk. "Take the trail that goes downhill," he said. "At least it'll be easier on the horses. The ranch is down in a hollow anyway, not uphill."

Fawn gave a haughty little grunt and spurred Virgy down the trail.

"What's the matter with her?" Will whispered to Miguel over his shoulder.

"I seldom understand girls," Miguel said. "And Fawn, never."

Will only gave the matter a few more glum thoughts before he found himself having to concentrate completely on guiding Cisco through what was now almost total darkness. The piñons and junipers had turned into bulky shadows on either side of them, and the trail was all but invisible beneath the horses' feet. Cisco slowed down on his own, and Will kept murmuring to him, "Easy now. Easy, boy." He wasn't certain whether it was himself or the horse he was reassuring.

The only thing he WAS sure of was that Fawn was still only a few yards ahead of him and that she had a clearer idea of where she was going than he did. Virgy's hooves clopped steadily on the dirt path, until they suddenly stopped and Fawn said, "Shhh!"

"What?" Will whispered.

"Shhh-*shhh!*" Fawn said.

She maneuvered Virgy backward so that she was beside Will. He could feel the stiffness in her as she reached over to tug his sleeve.

"Don't make a sound," she whispered. "Just look down there."

She didn't even point but just moved her head slightly. Will held his breath and peered through the dark.

At first he didn't see anything and was about to bop Fawn on the head for making him look like an idiot. But then something moved—a shadow—a shadow with form.

Whatever—or whoever—it was appeared to be climbing down from another form, probably a horse. For a second it disappeared into the shadows, and then Will saw it again, this time pulling something.

"What's that?" he whispered.

"Looks like a gate," Fawn said.

"What gate? Where are we?"

"I think that is a back gate to Señor T.'s property." That came from Miguel, who had edged up beside him on Hilachas.

"There's someone else!" Fawn hissed.

"We gotta get closer," Will said.

"Follow me," Fawn said. "And don't make any noise."

Will nodded and, never taking his eyes from the shadowy figures and their horses at the gate, gently urged Cisco forward. The horse seemed to be able to tell that Will wanted him to walk carefully, and his hooves were silent in the dirt.

Fawn led them behind a clump of three piñons that formed a fluffy wall on a slight rise, just above the gate. From there, Will could see that the gate had been pulled out from an adobe wall with an arch over it. There was even an adobe out-building right below them which butted against the wall. Miguel was right; this was clearly part of Mr. T.'s ranch.

"We could get down behind that building and see better," Will whispered to Fawn.

She nodded, though she still put her finger up to her lips, and then led the way in and out among the trees toward the wall. Although Will couldn't hear Miguel behind him or Fawn out in front, the creaking of his saddle and the breath coming from Cisco's nostrils crashed in his ears, and he was sure whoever was lurking around Mr. T.'s gate could hear and would turn on them any second.

It's the cattle rustlers, he thought. *They're back to take more cattle—I know it!*

Almost as if he'd heard his thoughts, a steer suddenly gave a mournful wail.

"Aw, hesh up," someone said.

Will felt the hair standing up on the back of his neck. The voice was rough as sandpaper and sounded as if it were being spit out of the corner of someone's mouth. It made Will want to shout something back at him.

But he waited, not even breathing, until he and Fawn and the horses were concealed behind the wall. From there, it was easy to see what was going on at the gate.

One man was on his horse, a kerchief tied around his nose and mouth and his hat lowered over his eyes, so that his face seemed to have no features at all. He had several head of cattle tethered to his horse and was waiting while the other man closed the gate. His horse stood to one side, head down, as if it were ashamed of the big, stupid cattle that lowed under their breaths and made no attempt to break away.

"They're stealing Mr. T.'s cattle!" Fawn whispered hoarsely. "We gotta get back and tell him!"

But Will shook his head, slightly at first, and then harder, until suddenly he was jabbing his heels into Cisco's sides.

I've had enough of not fighting back! he thought as Cisco burst forward. *I've had enough!*

"You go get Mr. T.," Will spat out over his shoulder. "I'm going after them!"

Cisco seemed to stretch himself out into one smooth line as he galloped after the thieves with Will hunkered down on his back. Though the men were obviously hurrying to put the ranch behind them, the cattle slowed them down. Will was on them before their dust had settled at the gate.

"Stop!" Will shouted. "Those are Mr. Tarantino's cattle!"

The man on the horse just ahead of him turned in the saddle and tilted his head back to see. For an instant, Will got a glimpse of his eyes, and in that flash he saw that they were crossed, as if the man were trying desperately to see his own nose.

It was enough of a surprise to make Will hesitate for a fraction of a second. In that same fraction, he could hear Fawn charging up behind him, and he saw the man dance his horse around, cattle and all, so that he was facing Will. His eyes were hidden again. There was only the hat pulled low over a bandit's bandana.

For the first time, Will realized he had absolutely no plan for what to do now. He shouted, "Hand over the cattle!" with all the anger that was boiling inside him, but it hung in the air like a puff of harmless smoke.

It must have seemed that way to the man, too, because he wheezed out a laugh—just before he let fly with a black-gloved hand that landed squarely in the middle of Will's chest.

It knocked a groan right out of Will, and he was on the ground before he could even feel himself leaving Cisco's back and falling through the air. The sound of a thud beside him told him that Fawn had been shoved off her horse too. The night was suddenly filled with the pounding of all manner of hooves, and Will rolled onto his stomach and covered his head, praying that none of them would come down on him.

And then it was suddenly silent. Will looked up. Even Cisco and Virgy had left them. Miguel and Hilachas were nowhere in sight.

"Where's Miguel?" Will said.

"He went back to get Mr. T.," Fawn said.

"At least *he* did what I told him to." He glared at Fawn.

"Fine," Fawn said. "Next time I'll leave you out here to get killed all by yourself."

"I'm wasn't gonna get killed! I was gonna get the cattle back!"

"And who stopped you?" Fawn said. "It sure wasn't me. Matter of fact, I probably could've got 'em if you hadn't charged right up yelling your head off."

"And how were you gonna do that, Miss Know-It-All?" Will said. "Never mind—where are the horses?"

"Soon as we got knocked off, they took off for the stables," Fawn said. "And that's where I'm goin' before we get in even more trouble."

She picked herself up off the ground and gave the seat of her pants a swat with each hand before she headed for the gate and neatly climbed over it. Once on the other side, she propped both arms on the top rail.

"You coming or not?" she said.

"In a minute," Will said. "Go on."

"You're not going after them, are you?" she said. He could see her eyes narrowing even in the darkness. "Don't you dare go after them without me, Will Hutchinson!"

"I'm not goin' anywhere," Will said, his teeth tight. "I just need a minute. Can't a fella have a minute alone?"

"Sure," Fawn said, flipping her braids over her shoulders. "You can have all the minutes you *want!*"

She marched off, head thrown back in a huff. Will groaned

and fell back onto the ground where he'd been dumped.

"God?" he said out loud when he was sure Fawn was out of earshot. "I'm about as mad as I know how to get! I feel like I'm gonna explode! I want to fight somebody! Everybody—all the bad guys are getting exactly what they want, and I can't fight back."

He rolled onto his stomach and dug his hands into his hair. He wasn't sure it was the right kind of prayer to be praying, but he couldn't hold it in. "God?" he said. "Would You please give me a fight I can win? Please? I'm sick of this, do You hear me? I'm sick of it!"

And then he pounded his fists into the dirt until they couldn't pound any more.

☦-✦-☦

Chapter Six

Will was still lying facedown in the dirt when he heard a horse approaching. Its footfalls were so calm and sure, he knew without looking up that it wasn't one of the thieves coming back. Even before he heard the voice say, "Will? Is that you, Son?" he knew it was Mr. T.

Will rolled over and sat up. For the first time he realized how hard and cold the ground was under him—and how ridiculous he must look covered in dust and shivering like a wet cat. Still, he didn't get up until Mr. T. dismounted his wheat-colored mare and started to squat beside him. It was something Will's dad would have done, and Will couldn't trust himself with it. He was sure he'd start bawling.

Instead, Will sprang to his feet and, folding his arms across his chest, scowled at the ground.

"I would have gone after them," Will said. "But Fawn messed it up, and they knocked us both off our horses and took off."

Mr. T. chuckled softly. "That's a little different from the version I heard, but it doesn't matter. As long as you kids are safe—"

"It does too matter!" Will said. "I shouldn't of just let 'em get away with your cattle! I shoulda fought back harder!"

Mr. T. was quiet for a long moment—so long, in fact, that Will wondered if he'd even heard what he said. Or if they were in trouble for keeping the horses out after dark. Or if he was trying to find a way to tell Will they wouldn't be able to ride anymore.

"I'm sorry we didn't get back on time," Will started to say.

But Mr. T. put his hand on Will's shoulder and gave it a firm squeeze.

"I tell you what," he said. "It's late and it's getting cold and you're probably hungry. Señora Otero has a pot of beans ready, so let's go in and have a bowl before your mother takes you kids home."

"What about the horses?" Will said. "We have to get 'em unsaddled and fed and—"

"The ranch hands are taking care of that this time. You kids need to get home and get to bed—there's school tomorrow."

"But we have to—"

"And speaking of school, I want you to stop in and see me when classes are over."

"Oh," Will said.

Friend or no friend, Mr. T. was still the principal, and being called to his office put a little fear in Will, no matter how many times they'd had *good* talks in there. Why couldn't Mr. T. just come out with it now and get it over with? And why wasn't Will allowed to *ask* him that?

Will shoved his hands into his pockets and nodded as he glowered at the toes of Mr. T.'s boots. "Okay," he said. "I'll be there."

But to himself he added, *But I don't have to like it.*

Being sullen seemed to be the only way he could keep from telling the whole world that he was sick of their turn-the-other-cheek, some-ditches-aren't-worth-dying-in, just-let-it-go thinking. If it weren't for the pastor and Mom and Mr. T., he would gladly be punching out every person who even looked like he— or she—was going to tell him to smile and make the best of it.

So all the way through a supper of beans and leftovers from Señora Otero's dinner the night before, and on the short drive back to Santa Fe, and even when his mother came in to tell him and Abe good night, Will answered questions with grunts and returned smiles with sulky frowns. When his mother offered her pinky to link with his—their substitute for a kiss—Will barely let his finger touch hers.

When the already-dim light was out, Will heard the cot Abe was sleeping on creak as the big kid sat up. Will pretended to be asleep already, but he couldn't ignore Abe's whisper, which was loud enough to bring the air raid warden down on them.

"Will?" he said.

Will grunted.

"Mad, Will?"

Turning over in the bed with an exasperated sigh, Will said, "I told you, I'm not mad at you. I'm mad at the stupid war, and that stupid moron at Hinkle's with the stupid clothes, and those stupid thieves that took Mr. T.'s cattle, and the stupid people that keep telling me to just keep smiling and keep trying and keep having faith when I want to *do* something about something!"

"Stupid," Abe said.

"Yeah," Will said. "Stupid."

That seemed to satisfy Abe, but it was a long time before Will could fall asleep, which made his mood the next day even more sour. It didn't help that when he looked in the bathroom mirror he saw a large black-and-blue goose egg on his forehead, compliments of the horse thief.

I even look like he won, he thought miserably.

By the time Will got to his first-period English class and dropped into his seat, his mood was black. His friend Neddie, who was in the desk next to his, peered at him through the smudges on his glasses and cocked his very large head so that it seemed in danger of toppling off of his toothpick of a neck.

"You collided with Mr. T. and banged your head on his belt buckle," he said.

Will rubbed the bruise on his forehead and scowled. That, however, didn't stop Neddie. He had more imagination than Walt Disney.

"You were driving your mother's motorcycle and you hit a bump and you went flying over the handlebars and landed on your head. Right on Palace Avenue."

"No," Will snapped.

"I know! You were out past curfew and you were trying to get home and the air raid warden caught you and smacked you over the head with a billy club."

"They don't even carry billy clubs," Will said.

"Then it was the *marshal person!*"

"No!" Will said.

Mrs. Torres looked over from the doorway where she was shooing the last of the students in before the bell, and Will slumped down in his seat.

"Shut up, Neddie," he whispered. "You're gonna get us in trouble."

Neddie nodded. His face was dark with daydreams. "Yeah," he said. "Mrs. Torres would probably slide those bamboo shoots under our fingernails and torture us with them."

Will buried his face in his *Adventures in World Literature* book. *Just let her try it,* he thought. *I'd show her a thing or two.*

And then he grunted. *Right. As if anybody would* let *me.*

His state of mind got no better as the day went on. In second-period math, old Mr. Marin called him to the board not once, but twice. It was probably because the aging teacher had forgotten he'd called on him the first time, but by the end of the period,

Will had himself convinced Mr. Marin was out to get him.

In third-period science, they had a substitute teacher who didn't refer to the list of lab partners on the desk, but paired Will up with a girl instead of letting him work with Miguel. She giggled through the entire experiment, and Will found himself thinking that the girl he'd almost run over with Cisco probably never giggled.

Why am I thinking that? he asked himself. He was so busy fighting *that* thought, he couldn't even eat the lunch Mom had packed for him. Neddie gladly wolfed down the streusel she had wrapped in waxed paper, while Miguel watched Will curiously.

"You are troubled, my friend," he said when Neddie had gone to try to wheedle another bottle of milk out of the cafeteria lady.

"Nah," Will said.

"Oh, yes. You are troubled."

"Why shouldn't I be?" Will said.

He spoke louder than he'd meant to, and three girls at the other end of the table looked at each other with wide eyes. That irritated Will even more, but he lowered his voice.

"See?" he said, stretching his neck across the table toward Miguel. "You can't even be in a bad mood around here. I want to *do* something, and everybody keeps telling me to pipe down and calm down and sit down."

Miguel was nodding, so Will kept going. "I'm sick of not fighting back," he said. "I just want to argue or fight—I wanna *win* something for a change!"

"Me, too." It was Neddie, back with a bottle of milk Will was pretty sure he'd taken when the cafeteria lady wasn't looking. "I wanna win one of those contests like on the radio. You know, like write a new jingle for Juicy Fruit gum and win a year's supply." His eyes sprang open behind the dirty film on his lenses. "Do you know how much gum that is? If you chewed it all, I bet it would be enough to hold a B-29 bomber together—"

"Neddie," Will said.

"Huh?"

"Shut *up!*"

The girls at the end of the table snatched up their lunches and ran. Miguel looked at Will with sympathy in his eyes, but Will wasn't sure he understood. He wasn't sure anybody did.

Fourth-period social studies was usually Will's favorite class, but he didn't have too much faith that it was going to cheer him up that day as he took his seat after lunch. He wasn't even sure he *wanted* to be cheered up, since that was the very thing everybody *else* seemed to want him to do. He grunted and scowled and glared his way through copying the New Mexico facts from the blackboard while Mrs. Rodriguez checked attendance.

"New Mexico was the 47th state to be admitted to the Union."

I would *live in a state that's behind all the other states.*

"The state gem is the turquoise."

Of course. It couldn't be a diamond or a ruby.

"The state vegetables are the chile and the pinto bean."

The state vegetables? Who cares *about vegetables? We couldn't have a state* soldier *or a state* slogan—*like "Nobody gives New Mexico the business!"?*

"The state flower is the yucca."

Flower. Oh, now that's *powerful.*

"The state bird is the roadrunner."

No wonder the Japanese and the Germans don't respect us! We have goony birds that run around like headless chickens for our mascots!

"Let's get those written down, class," Mrs. Rodriguez said as she closed the roll book. "I have something interesting to tell you."

Will resisted the urge to roll his eyes as he scratched down the last of the New Mexico facts. He liked Mrs. Rodriguez, but she was one teacher he never fooled around with. She had eyes that didn't miss a thing and ears that could pick up the sound of someone even thinking about cheating. Even now, as she fingered the pale blue beads that exactly matched her earrings, she was studying Will with her raven-black eyes as if she somehow sensed that he was about to roll his eyes. Will tried to look interested.

"Your next project is going to be a three-dimensional one," she said.

Neddie's hand shot up.

"I will explain what three-dimensional is," Mrs. Rodriguez said, "if given the opportunity."

"I know what it is," Neddie said. "It isn't flat, like people on a movie screen, but it has sides, like people in real life." He shoved his glasses up on his nose. "Wouldn't it be keen if they could make movies that were three-dimensional? Then King Kong would be so real and people would be fainting in their seats and running, screaming, from the theater—"

"Thank you, Neddie," Mrs. Rodriguez said. "I think we get the point. May I go on?"

"Oh, sure," Neddie said.

Will couldn't resist looking at Miguel and rolling his eyes. Miguel nodded as he smothered a smile.

"As Neddie has pointed out," Mrs. Rodriguez went on, "a three-dimensional project would be one in which you show what you have learned not by writing about it or drawing a picture of it on paper, but by representing it with a model or a—"

"Like bringing in your train set instead of drawing pictures of trains!" Neddie burst out.

Mrs. Rodriguez just looked at him. "Sorry," Neddie said. "Go on."

"No more outbursts, Edward," Mrs. Rodriguez said, "or you will be learning about this project after school."

Who wants to learn about it at all? Will thought. Of course, that might be better than meeting Mr. T. after school.

"The theme for your project will be 'Treasures of New Mexico,'" Mrs. Rodriguez said. "You will work with a partner and choose any subject that you think relates to that theme. The two of you will then build a model or create a diorama or in some way represent, in three-dimensional form, that subject."

She crossed the room at a brisk walk, her short, stocky body gliding across the floor, and pointed to three shoeboxes, each one filled with a display of rocks or homemade adobe buildings or miniature Spanish-style furniture.

"Here are some examples," she said. "But I will expect yours to be of much higher quality than these, because this year, all of the projects will be put on exhibit in the gymnasium, and there will be prizes for the best ones."

"What kind of prizes?" Neddie said, hand waving. "Like a year's supply of Juicy Fruit?"

While Mrs. Rodriguez sorted that out, amid giggles from the girls and groans from the boys, Will turned to Miguel.

"Will you be my partner?" Miguel said.

"Yeah," Will said. "And Miguel—we are gonna beat the pants off of everybody in this school."

For the first time that day, Will felt a smile spread over his face. Finally, something he could fight for—and win.

✝ ✝ ✝

Chapter Seven

*I*t felt so good to have a victory to think about that might actually be within his reach, Will was whistling as he headed down the main hall for the front door of the school that afternoon.

"Now that's more like it," somebody said to him.

Will looked up quickly to see Mr. T. standing in his office doorway. He was lazily fingering his string tie, but his eyes, Will knew, took in the scene in one sweep.

"Hi!" Will said. "I was just coming in to see you! Y'know, just like you asked me to."

"Good," Mr. T. said, his eyes still bright on Will. "The way you were charging toward that door, I thought you'd forgotten."

Will thought about denying it, but he decided it was pointless. Mr. T. had a way of seeing through kids as if their skin were made of windowpanes.

"Come on in," Mr. T. said. "Let's talk."

It was the last thing Will wanted to do. He'd been feeling good about the social studies project, and he wanted to stay that way. Talking to Mr. T. was only going to stir up all the things he was mad about—and couldn't do a thing to change.

But he followed Mr. T. dutifully into his office and took the chair made out of a saddle that Mr. T. pointed to as he rummaged through his desk. He pulled out two big Tootsie Rolls and tossed one to Will, who decided it would be rude not to eat it.

Mr. T. waited until Will had a mouthful of candy goo before he said, "So, Will—I wanted to talk to you about something that concerns me."

Will wanted to reassure him that there was absolutely nothing to be concerned about when it came to him, but to do that would have meant opening his mouth and letting Tootsie Roll juice roll down his chin. So he just nodded.

"It has to do with battles." Mr. T. seemed to be having no trouble talking and downing his Tootsie at the same time. Someday, Will told himself, he was going to have to ask him how he did that. But right now, as serious as Mr. T.'s eyes were, obviously wasn't the time.

"I get the impression," Mr. T. went on, "that there are a number of battles that you would like to fight. Am I right?"

Will nodded, but cautiously.

"Some of them, of course, you can't. I know you'd like to go over to the Pacific and pull your father out of that prison camp with your own hands, and then the two of you take on Iwo Jima and Okinawa and work your way right into Japan."

It was so like daydreams Will had had, he almost choked on what was left of his candy. He nodded again.

"That has to be frustrating for you. It's frustrating for all of us. And then, of course, there's your friend Abe, who's waiting to hear if he can be legally adopted and if his parents are still alive or have been killed at the hands of Hitler. And your friend Fawn, whose father is fighting his way across Germany, risking his life every day—"

A storm was brewing again in Will's head. *You can stop any time now,* he wanted to say. *I hear enough of this over and over in my own mind. I don't need you reminding me!*

Mr. T., however, went on. "And your mother tells me that your latest attempt to help with the war effort was thwarted by that character down at Hinkle's." Mr. T. chuckled. "He has quite the wardrobe, doesn't he? I actually saw him in a pair of Bermuda shorts one day. Bermuda shorts and sneakers, right downtown."

By now Will could talk, but he just muttered, "Uh-huh," and wished Mr. T. would get to the point.

"Then I step in and refuse to allow you to go after my cattle rustlers," Mr. T. said. "You must feel as if you're being foiled at every turn."

That seemed to require an answer, so Will nodded. But what was the point? Mr. T. couldn't change anything. Nobody could change anything without a fight.

"Losing battles," Mr. T. said, and then waited.

"Sir?" Will said.

"You must feel like you're fighting losing battles all the time."

"Kind of, I guess," Will said.

"But you don't have to lose every battle, my friend. Not if you choose your battles carefully."

"Choose them?" Will said. "I don't get to choose them!"

"Sure you do. The battles are there, but God gave you the freedom to choose which ones you're going to fight and which ones you're going to either walk away from or let someone else fight, with you praying for them."

"I need an example," Will said. He fingered the last of the Tootsie Roll out of his teeth so he wouldn't get caught not able to talk again.

"You can choose to throw rotten tomatoes at Hinkle's

because his clerk won't contribute to the war effort, or you can choose to pray for him. You can decide to go after my cattle rustlers on your own and possibly get yourself hurt, or you can decide to pray that I'll handle it the best way I know how."

"Those aren't really choices," Will said. "If I do throw tomatoes or go after the rustlers, I'll get in trouble."

"But you seem to be choosing to fight those battles inside yourself instead of surrendering them. That'll get you into worse trouble." Mr. T. put his hand to his chest. "In here."

Will felt his eyes narrowing. "Are you talking about turning the other cheek?"

"That's one way of putting it," Mr. T. said. He looked impressed. "You've been reading your Bible."

Will shook his head. "The sermon Sunday. You missed it."

"From the look on your face, I take it you don't think I missed that much."

"I just don't get it. I feel like a big sissy just sitting around letting everybody else fight the battles."

"That isn't being a sissy; it's being wise. You think it's brave to throw yourself into battles you can't possibly win?"

"But how do I know I can't win unless I try?" Will said.

"Yes, sometimes you have to try and fail in order to know you can't win. But you tried to go after the cattle rustler and he pushed you off your horse. Don't you think it would be foolish to try that again?"

"I guess," was all Will could say.

Mr. T. leaned forward, resting his forearms on his knees and entwining his long fingers. "You don't have to wait until you get shoved out of your saddle to know which battles to fight, son," he said. "That's what prayer is for—to ask God to help you choose. I know you know how to pray. You've proven that over and over these last few months." He waited for Will to meet his eyes before he added, "But there's going to have to be a lot of cheek-turning in the process. If God doesn't want you to fight a battle, you have to walk away. I know it sounds like I'm preaching, but with Reverend Bud gone, I felt like I needed to step in. You understand, don't you?"

Will nodded, partly because he couldn't be rude to Mr. T., and partly because he was glad Bud *wasn't* there to preach to him. He probably would just be getting warmed up about now. Bud was swell, but he never let Will get away with anything when it came to God.

"Now then," Mr. T. said as he stood up and parked his hands lazily in his pockets. "It seems to me there are some horses to be ridden this afternoon." He grinned and added, "And Señora Otero is cooking again."

Will ignored that part. His mouth was dropping open over the first part. "We can still ride?" he said.

"Of course."

"But what about last night?"

"I have my ranch hands keeping watch on both gates, all pastures," Mr. T. said. "We won't have a repeat of last night—especially since you kids are never going to stay out after dark again."

"Right!" Will said. He grinned, and he was suddenly a little sorry he'd pouted through their entire conversation. He put his hand out for Mr. T. to shake it. "Thanks, Mr. T.," he said. "You're swell, really."

"In spite of my preaching?"

"No, that's okay," Will said, stammering a little. "I mean, it's like your job or something, right?"

"Something like that," Mr. T. said. He gave Will's hand a final squeeze and patted his back. "Now go exercise those horses or they'll start looking like me. Señora Otero's cooking is going to fatten me up."

He didn't have to tell Will twice. As soon as he was beyond the office door, he shot outside like a launched missile and nearly mowed Miguel down on the front steps.

"Let's go!" he said. "The horses are waiting!"

He towed Miguel home on the back of his bike, and the two of them waited impatiently for Fawn to get home from St. Catherine's School and change out of her uniform and into one of Will's old shirts and a pair of rolled-up jeans. Only because Mom insisted did she throw on a jacket, too.

"It's only March," Mom said. "It isn't shirt-sleeve weather quite yet."

Already feeling Cisco galloping under him, Will rode his bike like the wind out to the ranch with Miguel holding on behind him and Fawn zipping out ahead, braids flying. It was the beginning of a routine that by Thursday they felt they'd been following forever.

As soon as school was out every day, they changed into riding clothes and took off on bikes for the ranch. They saddled up the horses, which by Tuesday they could do without any help from Gabby, tucked Señora Otero's corn bread spiced with green chilies into their saddlebags, along with bottles of water, and headed out for parts unknown with Cisco and Virgy and Hilachas.

But each day their ride was a little different, because each day, Will found something new to gaze at, something he'd never really noticed before. Something about being on horseback, without grown-ups, gave him the freedom to observe.

Like the way they could climb right into the caves which erosion had formed in the cliff walls. And the way the sun baked the ground where they sat to eat their snack and talk. And the way jackrabbits sat straight up to listen to the kids' chatter before they shot off among the clumps of buffalo grass.

Will had never really watched a roadrunner before, and he and Miguel and Fawn rolled on the ground laughing at the way one would dash down the trail, head lowered, tail raised, feet reaching out in a stretched-out-like-a-rubber-band stride while it streaked along.

He decided he'd like to try trout fishing in one of the streams they found. And maybe climb all the way to the top of a big rock mesa they discovered. And even go looking for silver. There was, after all, some sparkly stuff in some of the rocks, so bright it blinded them when the sun hit it.

Miguel told them it was called pyrite, which wasn't worth anything but sometimes meant there might be valuable rock nearby.

That was when Will got what he called his brilliant idea.

"What if we found gold, Miguel?" he said.

Miguel shook his head. "There has been no gold in New Mexico for a very long time, my friend. It is said there was never much to begin with."

Will pointed to a pile of black dirt the size of a small mountain which had obviously been dug from somewhere. "Then what's all that from?" he said. "Not just coal mines."

"No. Those may be the outcroppings from the old turquoise mines at Los Cerrillos."

"Oh, yeah," Fawn said. "I know about that. You have to dig to get turquoise for all that jewelry they sell at the Governor's Palace. They mostly make pottery on my pueblo, but some Indians—"

"That's it!" Will said.

"That's what?" Fawn said.

"That's what we can do for our New Mexico's Treasures project, Miguel! We can do a model about finding turquoise. Y'know, how you dig for it and stuff."

"But you don't *know* how to dig for it," Fawn said.

"So we find out—that's what you do in school." Will left off the word "moron," but Fawn caught it in his eyes and glared at him. He was *never* going to understand girls.

After that, having a goal made their afternoon rides even more of an adventure. During social studies class, Mrs. Rodriguez let Will and Miguel go to the library to look up whatever they could find about turquoise mining. Then on their rides after school, they tried to apply what they were learning. Some of it was a little tough to do.

One book told them that the early Indians would build a fire against the rock where they thought turquoise might be and then throw water on the rock. The rock would then shatter and they would see a seam of fresh turquoise, "Like a blue stream of water," the book said. When they tried it in one of the small caves that looked something like a picture Will had seen, all they got was a face full of smoke, not to mention the fact that they flushed out a whole family of bats in the process.

"I don't see any turquoise," Fawn said when the smoke had cleared and they were all staring up at a charred rock wall.

"The rock didn't break," Will said. "Besides, we don't even know if there's any turquoise in there. We gotta keep reading."

Another book told them that rough turquoise looked like a plain brown stone with a vein of turquoise through it. It wasn't finger-sliding smooth like the polished stones the Indian women sold. The kids spent hours hunting for such rock, running their fingers over cave walls until they were raw, but with no luck.

By Friday, they'd combed dozens of caves, and Will felt like he was becoming an expert. He could spout off words he hadn't known a week before.

"Remember," he told them that afternoon, "turquoise can occur in seams, veins, or nodules."

"What's a nodule?" Fawn said. "It sounds ugly."

"It's like a wart or a lump or somethin'," Will said.

"Oh—then it *is* ugly."

"It wasn't uncommon during the 1880s to find veins as thick as three inches," Will said.

Fawn gave him a look. "You're starting to sound like some-body smart."

"I *am* smart."

"No—I mean, *really* smart. Teacher smart."

"I wish that it were the 1880s now," Miguel said. He stood back from the wall they were examining and rubbed the back of his neck. "I am tired from looking and looking."

"Me, too," Fawn said. "Can't we do something else for a while?"

Will had to admit, he was getting a little weary of searching for something he wasn't so sure was really there. But while they were concentrating on the turquoise, it kept him from thinking so much about things that made him mad. He hadn't wanted to punch someone in the nose since they'd started their search.

Still, it *was* getting boring, and the way Fawn was eyeing him, he knew if he didn't find something interesting to do, she was going to jump him, just to liven things up a little.

"Okay," Will said. "What about hide and seek? There oughta be some good hiding places around here."

"Yes!" Fawn said, eyes gleaming.

"But no fair going farther than this area; no going over the hill or way down in the canyon."

"We'll stay within shouting distance," Fawn said. "And this cave will be home base."

"Who's It?" Will said.

"You are!" Fawn said. And with a shout of "Come on, Miguel!" she disappeared through the mouth of the cave.

"Sorry, my friend," Miguel said with his slow smile. "But you will find us quickly."

"Right," Will said. "I'll be ready for false teeth or something before I ever find Fawn. That's okay, though. She'll get tired of being in hiding and give me a clue."

Miguel nodded and slipped out of the cave. Will turned his

face to the wall and, covering his face with his hands, began to count loudly.

"One—two—three—" *Why did I pick this game? I'm lousy at it. Fawn always wins,* "four—five—six—" *Of course she does—she's an Indian, for Pete's sake.* "Seven—eight—nine—" *Maybe Mr. T. had a point—I gotta choose my battles more carefully—*"10—11—12—"

He only counted to 20 before he yelled, "Here I come, ready or not!" and emerged into the bright sunlight outside the cave. Virgy and Hilachas were chewing contentedly on some rabbit brush where they were tied, and Cisco was scratching the side of his face on a stalk of *cholla* cactus.

"If somebody runs to base, you gotta tell me," he said to them.

They barely looked at him and kept munching.

"Here I come, ready or not!" he shouted again.

There were no telltale pebble falls or rustlings of branches. Will shaded his eyes with his hand and looked around.

There were a lot of caves and indentations in the rocks, but those would be too obvious, especially for Fawn.

I have to think like her, Will thought, and then he grunted. *That'll be the day, when I can think like* any *girl. They're all loony.*

He did know, however, that Fawn was a good climber. She'd gotten him up many a tree that he couldn't get down from, while she skittered to the ground like a chipmunk. Will looked around again and saw a sturdy-looking cottonwood, just beyond the crest of a little hill.

She's probably up there waiting to drop down on me, he thought. *That would be just like her.*

The only way to surprise her was to creep from one juniper bush to the next until he was maybe four feet from the tree. By the time he told her he spotted her, he could be right at the base of it, ready to tag her the minute she hit the dirt.

Crouching down like a wildcat, Will moved silently behind the first juniper and waited, listening. There was no sound of Fawn dropping to the ground. He got to the next one and then the next, with still no stirring from Fawn. That either meant she hadn't seen him, or she wasn't up there.

She could be running for home base this very minute from someplace else, Will thought. *I better make sure she's up there before I waste any more time.*

He tried to get high enough to see over the juniper, but that made him too visible if she *was* up there. If he could just back up a little. . . .

Tilting his head back so he could keep an eye out for movement in the tree, Will moved slowly backward, one step at a time. No Fawn.

She fooled me again! Will thought. *Next time, we're playing a different game.*

But she could be at the very top. If he went back just a little farther. . . . Will put his foot behind him—but there was no ground there. The lack of any place to set his heel down threw him off balance, and suddenly he was falling.

His last thought was a hope that Fawn didn't see him landing on his backside. But he didn't land. He just kept falling and falling, deeper and deeper into blackness, until he landed with a thud on something hard. Around him, there was nothing but darkness.

✜ ⋅✜⋅ ✜

Chapter Eight

*P*anic grabbed Will like a large, squeezing hand. He could barely breathe as he got to his feet and frantically groped around with his hands. They didn't have to stretch far before they hit on hard rock, but it was so black where he was, he couldn't see it even when he pressed his face close to it.

Heart pounding like a trip hammer, Will threw his head back and looked upward. He could just see a crack of sky, enough to let in light that seemed to stop just out of reach of his hands as he thrust them up.

I'm in a tunnel—going down! he thought. *It bends right there, where I can see sky—*

He looked down and stomped his feet. The rock under him was solid. *Thank You, God,* he thought. *Thank You that it stops here.*

But he knew he might as well have fallen all the way to the center of the earth, for all the good it had done him to land here. It was a good 10 feet to the bend in the tunnel, and who knew how far up from there.

Ten feet.

Will put his hands up to his head and tried to think. Why was that number familiar? Was it something he'd read while he was studying about the turquoise mines?

And then he had it: *Mining regulations state that a shaft no less than 10 feet deep shall be sunk in the vein or lode.*

"I'm in a mine shaft," he whispered. And then his voice burst from his throat: "Help! Somebody. Fawn! Miguel! I'm in a mine shaft. Help me!"

But he had to stop and put his hands over his ears. His words only bounced from wall to wall, shouting back at him.

It's no use anyway, he thought as he stared up at the open-ing. *They're not gonna find me forever. I'm It—why would they look for me? And how are they gonna get me out of here when they* do *find me?*

Suddenly it seemed as if the walls were closing in on him, and he was sure he couldn't breathe. Gasping for air, Will jumped and tried to grab at the opening. But he would have had to be four feet taller than he was to even touch it, much less get a handle on it.

"I can't breathe!" he said. "I'm gonna die in here! God—don't let me die!"

"You *are* gonna die if you wear yourself out yelling."

Will froze, his eyes glued to the opening. Had he heard a voice, or was he already losing his mind?

"Who's there?" he said.

"Me," said a female voice. "Now shut up so I can help you."

"Get Fawn and Miguel!" Will cried, jumping up again to try to reach the voice. "Tell them to go get Mr. T. or the ranch hands!"

"Do you really want all those people to know what a clumsy ox you are?"

"I just want to get out of here!"

"Then shut your pie hole and listen to me. I can get you out."

"Who are you?" Will said.

There was a laugh, a cackle that reminded Will of a chicken. "Does it matter?" she said. "You don't have too many choices, fella."

"Oh," Will said. There was something about her voice that made him less afraid. He hugged his arms around himself and said, "Okay, what do I do? You have to hurry—I can't breathe."

She cackled again. "For somebody that can't breathe, you're sure doing a lot of gum-flapping down there. There's enough air for you to last a couple of days."

"A couple of days!?"

"But if you would stop screeching about it, I can get you out in a few minutes."

"How?"

"I'm going to climb down to that bend in the shaft. It forms a little bit of a ledge. You must have bounced right through that." She laughed, more softly this time. "I didn't even ask you—are you all right? Do you think you broke any bones or anything?"

"No," Will said. "Just a little sore." He hoped his voice sounded steadier now. He was beginning to feel embarrassed. *Thank the Lord I* didn't *break any bones,* he thought. *Then I'd really feel like a sissy.*

"It'll take me a minute to get that far, so don't go wacky on me," she said.

Will could hear pebbles coming loose up above him and pattering down the wall of the shaft.

"Wait!" he said.

"Now what?"

"How are we gonna get back up from the ledge? And how are you gonna get *me* up to the ledge? It must be 10 feet!"

"I'm Superman. Make that Superwoman."

"*What?*"

"I have a rope, simple head."

There was more sliding of gravel. By now Will's eyes had adjusted to the darkness enough that he could see the walls around him. He watched anxiously, sure that any minute there was going to be a cave-in and he would be buried alive.

"Wait!" he said.

"For crying out loud! What do you want? I'm trying to perform a rescue here!"

"Why don't you just lower the rope from the top? Why are you coming down?"

"Because in the first place the rope isn't long enough, and in the second place I'm afraid you'd go crackers and I'd have to come down for you after all."

"I'm not going crackers," Will said. In spite of his fear, he could feel his cheeks going crimson. This girl, whoever she was, could tick him off faster than Fawn could—and that was saying something.

"Then be quiet and let me concentrate," she said.

"Why do you have to concentrate? What's wrong?"

He heard a loud sigh. When he looked up toward it, the opening at the bend in the shaft was filled with a dark form.

"The only thing that's wrong is your mouth. It seems to have a malfunction. It won't close."

Will gritted his teeth together and said through them, "It's closed."

"Good. Now, I can see you, but you probably can't really see me, so I'm going to throw the end of this rope right to you. It'll hit you in the chest, so be ready to grab it."

"Okay," Will said, and then to be on the safe side, he thrust his chest out as far as he could. Something hit it, dead center, and he grabbed for it. It went tight as soon as he got his hands around it.

"Good," said the girl above. "At least you haven't gone completely off your rocker. Now, tie the rope around your waist. Use a double knot—"

"I know!" Will said. With a lifeline to sunlight in his hand, it was time to start saving face a little.

With shaking fingers, he wrapped the rope around him and knotted it—three times. Then he gave it a yank to make sure it was secure.

"Yikes!" the girl said. "Would you warn me next time before you do that? You just about pulled me down there with you. *Then* we'd be in a fix."

Yeah, Will thought. *Then I'd have to listen to you making wisecracks until we both died!*

To his surprise, she cackled again. "I take it you wouldn't like that too much."

"No," Will said. "As a matter of fact, I wouldn't."

"Okay, I have the rope tied off to a rock up here so it isn't going anywhere."

"You sure?"

"Unless we suddenly have an earthquake or something, yeah, I'm sure."

"Okay."

"I can't pull you up by myself," she said.

"I thought you were Superwoman."

"Yeah, well, I left my cape in a phone booth. So you're gonna have to get yourself so that your feet are on one wall and your shoulders are on the other, and then with me pulling from up here and you walking yourself up, you'll be able to get up here. It gets more narrow as you go up, so it'll get easier."

Will's heart raced in his ears. "Say that again," he said.

She repeated it for him—twice. "Come on. You can do it," she said. "Anybody with a mouth as smart as yours can pull this off."

"What if I fall?"

"You fell all the way down there from the top and you didn't kill yourself, right?"

"Oh. Yeah."

Will felt his cheeks burning again. He wanted to say, *What if I keep falling? What if I never get up there?* But he refused to suffer any more humiliation. He pushed his shoulders against one wall of the cave and then put up one foot and then the other on the opposite wall.

"I'm ready," he called up to the girl. "What do I move first, my feet or my shoulders?"

"Shoulders," she said. "That way all the blood won't run to your head." There was the cackle again. "Although it probably wouldn't hurt you any."

Will didn't ask her what *that* was supposed to mean, though he wanted to. Instead, he slid his shoulders up the wall, and then braced himself and walked his feet up the other side. Between steps, he checked the rope.

"It's still holding," she said. "You sure aren't the trusting type, are you?"

"I was just checking," Will said, gritting his teeth again. "You would too, if you were down here."

"But I wouldn't *be* down there, because I know to watch where I'm going when I'm around mine shafts."

Will made a face at her which he knew she couldn't see and continued to grunt and push his way toward her. By the time he was almost there, his body was nearly vertical. It was hard to hold on with just his shoulders, so he put his hands up to brace himself. Another, warmer hand grabbed his wrists and then a second one. They pulled and tugged at him until he was waist high into the opening.

"Scramble up!" she said. "Throw your leg up!"

Will did, and he was suddenly on a ledge, 10 feet above where he'd been before but still a good seven feet from daylight.

"Yeah, you still have to climb some more," the girl said. "But I never said it was going to be easy."

For the first time, Will was able to look her full in the face. What he saw was a square jaw and shiny eyes and a mane of dark hair.

"It's you!" he said.

She nodded.

"I mean, you're the one that I—"

"Almost trampled with your horse? Yeah, it's me."

She didn't seem at all surprised that Will was who he was. And even in the half-light, he could tell she wasn't as embarrassed as he was.

"I guess if you'd known who it was down there you wouldn't have rescued me," Will said.

"Oh, I knew who it was," she said. "I saw you fall in."

"From where?" Will said.

"From that tree you were gaping at like a baboon. And by the way, the girl's behind a pile of rocks just up the hill and the boy's lying down under some pine trees. At least they were last time I saw them. They're probably back at home base by now, wondering where *you* are—so I guess we better get out of here, right?"

Will knew he was staring at her, just as she'd said, like a baboon. But he couldn't stop himself. She knew everything.

"You'd better close your mouth," she said. "Or a bat's liable to fly into it."

"Were you spying on us?" Will said.

"Let's just say I was observing," she said. "Now do you want to get out of here or not? If not, I'll just go. These holes give me the creeps."

"No—I wanna go!" Will said.

He jerked for the rope, nearly falling off the ledge and tumbling through the opening again.

"Look, I'm only going to do this once," the girl said. "After that, if you're stupid enough to fall again, you're on your own."

"Let's go," Will said tightly. *And then I'm gonna run as far away from you as I can!*

"All right," she said. "I'm going to take the rope up to the top and tie it off again and then you do the same thing you did down there—shoulders—feet—"

"Got it," Will said quickly. He glanced toward the top of the shaft. "But how are you going to get up there if the rope isn't tied off?"

"I can do it without the rope," she said.

Will straightened his shoulders. "Well, I probably could, too."

The girl cackled long and loud.

"What's so funny?" Will said.

"Until five minutes ago you were a candidate for a strait-jacket. Suddenly you're—"

"Superman," Will said.

The girl looked at him blankly for a second, and then she grinned, a smile so big he could practically see her molars.

"Okay, you got me," she said. "But just this once, why don't you let me do the free climb and you use the rope?" She patted him on the shoulder. "You've had a rough day."

"Next time, then," Will said. "Next time I'll show you I can do it without the rope."

"Next time you fall into a mine shaft and try to kill yourself?" she said dryly. "I'll think about it."

Then with a toss of her mane, she wedged herself between the walls and walked herself up as if she were strolling down the street. It made Will determined to go up just as fast. As soon as she had tied off the rope above, he hiked himself up between the walls and promptly slid back down to the ledge, landing on his bottom with his feet sticking up in one direction and his head and shoulders in the other.

"Everything all right down there?" the girl called down.

"Yeah, everything's fine!" Will said. He scrambled up and tried the wedging again, this time with better results. Huffing like a large train engine, he wriggled his way to the top, with only a faint hope that he looked as tough doing it as she did.

If he did, she didn't say. She merely reached down and untied the rope from his waist, looped it over her shoulder, and said, "So long. And be careful from now on, would you? I might not be around next time."

Then she turned on her heel and started off.

"Hey," Will said. The thought that *he* was going to run away from *her* faded like a bad idea.

She stopped and looked over her shoulder, one eye hidden behind her curtain of hair.

"Thanks," Will said. "Do you want—"

"You don't have to pay me," the girl said, and started to move on again.

"No, I was just gonna say—me and my friends have some snacks. If I could find them, you could—"

She turned around to face him. Some of the merriment was gone from her eyes.

"You know what—don't tell your friends," she said.

"Tell them what?"

"Don't tell anyone that you ever saw me. Unless you tell them I was your rescuing angel—then nobody will believe you anyway." Her voice still had that dry wit crackling in it, but she looked hard at him. "Is it a deal?"

"Sure, I guess," Will said. "But I don't see why—"

"You don't need to see," she said. "Except where you're going. Don't drop into any more mine shafts—because I won't be there to save you."

Then Will watched, bewildered, as she turned to walk away.

✢ ✢ ✢

Chapter Nine

*W*ait!" Will said.

The girl stopped and turned, folding her arms impatiently across her chest. "What?" she said.

"I don't get it."

"You don't have to 'get it.' You just have to promise you won't tell anybody you ever saw me up here."

For the first time, Will saw what looked like fear flash through her eyes.

"Why?" he said.

"Why?" The girl looked surprised. "Well—because I said so."

"Big deal," Will said.

"Because I just saved your life, simple head!"

She did have a point there, but Will pushed on.

"I might keep it a secret," he said, "if you tell me your name."

"I'm not going to tell you my name!" she said.

"Then I'm not going to promise anything," Will said.

Her dark eyes narrowed. "You really are a smart aleck, aren't you?"

"Yeah, I guess I am."

She surprised him by smiling. "I actually like a smart aleck. It's been a long time since I've talked to one."

"Actually, it's not smart aleck, it's smart *Will*," he said. "Nice to meet you—?"

"O.," she said.

"O. what?" Will said.

"Just call me O."

"What the devil kind of name is that?"

"Don't push it," she said. "I'm the one who just fished you out of a mine shaft, remember?"

Will glanced over at the offensive, gaping opening and stifled a shiver. "What *is* that, anyway?" he said.

"It's an old turquoise mine," she said. "I guess they finally decided there wasn't enough in there to bother with so they stopped digging. Lucky for you."

"We've been looking all over for turquoise," Will said.

O. shook her head and pointed to the large pile of black dirt Will and Fawn and Miguel had wondered about.

"You're better off digging in the tailings for whatever they might have missed. Nobody really mines for turquoise here anymore."

"Oh," Will said.

"Mostly they just mine potash, which, I admit, isn't as interesting."

"It doesn't sound like a treasure, that's for sure," Will said. "It has to be a treasure."

"What does?"

"Whatever we put in our project." Will shrugged. "It's for school."

O. sat down on a clear spot on the ground and plucked a piece of buffalo grass. "What school do you go to?"

"Harrington," Will said. *Fawn and Miguel should be looking for me by now*, he thought. *I really oughta go.* But he felt a little awkward standing up with her sitting down, so he dropped down beside her. That suddenly felt awkward, too, as if he didn't know what to do with his arms, which seemed to be growing longer by the minute. "What school do you go to?" he said.

She looked around, like she was afraid someone would hear her, and said, "I don't go to school."

"How come?" Will said.

"I'm taught at home."

"I used to have that, too. I like school better, though. Doesn't it get boring, just you and your mom?"

"It's not my mom, it's my—" She stopped and stuck a piece of buffalo grass into her mouth.

"It's your who?"

"It's my none of your business," she said, lips pressed around the grass. She pulled it out. "So—tell me about what they're doing in school these days. What's this project you're doing?"

Will launched into an explanation of Mrs. Rodriguez's assignment and the contest for prizes and the progress he and Miguel had made so far, with Fawn's help. He felt less and less awkward as he talked, especially since O. seemed to be hanging on his every sentence the ways kids hung onto monkey bars.

As she listened, O. leaned back on her elbows, once again chewing the buffalo grass like a mountain girl but following Will's words with the eyes of a scholar. When he finished his spiel about the project, he said, "So, where do you live, anyway? I didn't know there were any houses up here."

O. gave him a sharp look. "There aren't," she said, still making herself sound only half serious. "And I don't live up here. I don't live anywhere."

"All right, all right," Will said. "I'm not gonna come spying on you the way you've been spying on us."

O. gave one of her cackles. "Y'know, at first I thought you

were kind of a clumsy oaf—running me down with your horse and falling into a hole. But you're pretty sharp in the head. Most people can't keep up with me—when I actually *have* a conversation with somebody, that is."

"What do you mean?" Will said. "Are you some kind of hermit or something?"

"Just about." Her eyes darted sharply to his. "But don't tell anybody that, either."

"I heard you the first 47 times you said not to say anything about you," Will said.

"Sorry." She tossed the half-chewed piece of grass aside. "Like I said, I don't have that many conversations, so I'm not so good at it anymore."

Will wanted to ask her *why* she didn't have anybody to talk to, but instead he said, "We come up here a lot."

"I know."

"What do you do, sit up in trees and watch us?"

"I see things," she said.

"So you could talk to us any time we're up here," Will said.

"You, yes. 'Us,' no."

"Huh?"

"I'll talk to you, but not the little Indian girl and the boy."

"Why not?" Will said, voice cracking as it rose. "They're my friends. Fawn is like my sister—she lives with me and my mom."

"I'm happy for you," O. said dryly. "But they're kids. I can't trust them."

"Then why trust me?" Will said.

"You sure like to argue, don't you?"

"A lot of people say that," Will said. "So answer the question: Why trust me?"

"Because I saved your life. It seems to me you owe it to me to keep your mouth shut."

"Yeah, but I don't see why—"

"Hey—Will!" someone called from down the hill. "Are you ever gonna come looking for us or what?"

Will grinned and crawled toward the crest of the hill. "I'm up here!" he called down.

He saw Fawn's head poke out from behind a juniper bush and watched her shade her eyes with her hand to squint up at him. He waved and then turned back to O.

"They've been hiding all this ti—" But he stopped.

O. had disappeared.

"What did you do, change home base?" Fawn said.

Her voice grew closer behind him, but Will didn't look back. He was on his feet, scanning the hills with his eyes. Although he probably could have spotted a lizard, as sparse as the terrain was, he didn't see O.

"What are you looking for?" Fawn said. "Miguel's coming up behind us."

"I'm not looking for Miguel," Will said. "I'm looking for—"

And then he stopped. O. had said not to tell anybody. Not even Fawn and Miguel.

"Who?" Fawn said.

"Uh—this snake I was chasing," Will said.

"We better get you home," she said. "The sun's getting to you; all the snakes are still in hibernation."

"Weel!" Miguel said as he reached the top of the hill, breathing hard. "Did you count to 500 or something?"

"Nah, he was too busy chasing imaginary snakes," Fawn said.

Will just shrugged. Lying wasn't one of his talents. He'd be lucky if he could just get Fawn to forget the whole thing.

"We better go," he said. "If we don't get back before dark, I don't think Mr. T. *or* Miguel's mom is gonna let us ride again. Hey, are the horses okay?"

"They've eaten so much grass they're probably going to blow up," Fawn said. "Next time we play a game, you have to follow the rules, Will. *No* more changing home base and—"

She rattled on as they went down the hill, mounted the horses, and headed for the ranch. Even Hilachas seemed in a hurry to get back to the barn and his supper, and Cisco snorted and tossed his head in anticipation of grain.

"Look at Virgy swishin' her tail!" Fawn said. "She's *all* excited!"

It would have been fun to play with the horses in their frisky mood, and Miguel and Fawn did, dancing across the desert and laughing at the sunset. But Will lagged behind, and every chance he got, when he knew they wouldn't see him, he glanced back, watching for O.

Why do I even care where she went? he thought. *She's just a dumb girl.*

Well, not dumb, exactly. Matter of fact, she's pretty smart. Smarter than me, probably. And frisky—like the horses.

And she said I was smart. She said I could keep up with her when mostly nobody else could.

But what "nobody else"? She said she never talks to any-body. She doesn't go to school.

She's scared for anybody to even know she lives up there— if *she does.*

Cisco snapped his head back, nickering loudly, and Fawn laughed.

"He gets pretty ornery when he's hungry, doesn't he?" she said.

"I guess," Will said vaguely.

"Just like you," she said.

"Uh-huh," Will said.

"I think Will's sick," he heard Fawn say to Miguel.

Will ignored her and tried to concentrate on keeping Cisco under control, pulling in on the reins so he would slow down and stop trying to ride right up Virgy's shanks. When Fawn had gotten several yards ahead of him, Will heard a hissing sound to his left. He looked over and down.

O. rose slowly from behind a rock, so that only her face showed. Before Will could say anything, she put her finger up to her lips. With the other hand, she pointed to the ground where she was crouched. As he watched, she mouthed the word, *Tomorrow*.

Will opened his mouth to speak, but she quickly put her finger to her lips again. Will nodded and pointed to the spot. She nodded back.

"Come on, slowpoke!" Fawn called out. "What are you doing back there?"

"Controlling my horse," he said. "Which is more than I can say for you."

Virgy was tossing her head against the reins Fawn was holding tightly as she waited for Will to catch up. Fawn made a face at him and fell in beside him as they rode on behind Miguel.

"Are you mad at me, Will?" she said.

"No more than usual," Will said.

"No. I mean it—you're acting funny."

"I'm fine," Will said. And for some reason, that actually felt like the truth.

✝ ✝ ✝

Chapter Ten

*O*nce they were back at the barn, as Will watched Cisco take big mouthfuls of grain and chase the pile of kernels around in the feeding tub with his nose, he thought about O. Why did he want to talk to her again? Why did he get butterflies in his stomach when he thought about her telling him to come back to that very spot tomorrow?

Cisco dipped his mouth into his water bucket, just up to his nose, and drank deeply through lips that seemed to be closed and smiling. Will knew he must look that same way, standing there not saying a word and yet smiling to himself.

I know what it is, he decided. *I can argue with her, and she doesn't tell me to hush up or turn the other cheek. She argues right back!*

And yet it wasn't like fighting, really. She wasn't Fawn, who would jump him if she felt like she was losing the argument, or Miguel, who always ended up agreeing with Will because he liked to keep the peace. And she wasn't like Mom or Mr. T., who thought they knew better than he did.

Maybe they do, he thought. *But about some stuff, I know I'm right. I know I have to* do *something—about something— before I do go crackers!*

After Fawn and Miguel left to get some hot cider from the kitchen to warm them up, Will stayed behind. Cisco, being the biggest of the three horses, was still eating, and with only the sound of his jaws munching in the quiet barn, Will could think more clearly.

I'm gonna go back and see O. tomorrow, he thought. *I'm just gonna have to find a way to do it without Fawn and Miguel—and without hurting their feelings.*

As much as they didn't understand him right now, especially Fawn, they hadn't really done anything wrong. They just didn't get it. And he had a suspicion that O. did.

First thing I gotta do is find out what her real name is, he thought. *Nobody's name is just "O."*

But then he decided the *very* first thing was to come up with a plan for tomorrow. By the time he and Abe crawled into their beds that night, he had it outlined in his mind.

"Horses?" Abe whispered when Will turned the light out.

"There are no horses here, pal," Will said. "Go to sleep."

"Will. Horses?"

"Yeah, I rode the horses today," Will said.

Abe sighed heavily, and Will felt a stab of guilt. He propped himself up on his elbow.

"We went without you because you don't even get out of school until almost dark," he said. Abe went to the Opportunity School which was for older kids who, like Abe, had some special problems with learning. "And besides, you're scared of the horses."

"Stupid," Abe said.

Will smothered a laugh. "They're not stupid, pal. But if you're afraid of them, that's okay."

"No. Abey stupid."

"What?" Will sat straight up in bed. "You're not stupid! Who told you that?"

"Stupid war. Stupid moron. Stupid Abey."

"Knock it off," Will said. "I never said *you* were stupid. I just said all those other things were stupid. You're *not* stupid for being scared of the horses."

"Stupid?"

"No!"

Will picked up his pillow and bit into it so he wouldn't yell at poor Abe. He couldn't help it, but he was about to drive Will into a tantrum.

"Abey," Abe whispered. "Horses. *Not* stupid."

Will removed the pillow from his mouth. "Right!" he said. "Now don't ever say that again."

"Abey. Horses."

"Yeah, you keep saying that," Will said.

It was a suggestion he regretted 15 minutes later when Abe was still repeating "Abey. Horses." Will bit down on the pillow until in another half hour, Abe finally drifted off.

I gotta get some sleep, Will thought, *or I'm not gonna get up in time.*

But it was still dark when Will woke up and looked at the clock. 4:30 A.M. That should give him time to get dressed, slip out on his bike, and get to the ranch before there was too much activity out there. No one had said none of them could ride alone, without other kids with them, but he didn't want to take any chances. And he didn't want O. to think he wasn't going to show up.

Will slid out of bed and tiptoed to the chair where he'd laid out his clothes the night before. A glance at the cot reassured him that Abe was still in a deep sleep.

He should be, Will thought. *He wore himself out saying "Abey. Horses."*

Will wriggled into his clothes and padded down the steps in his socks, holding his boots in his hand. He was careful not to step on any of the spots where the stairs tended to creak. One false move and he'd have Mom to deal with. She had never said they couldn't ride solo either, but he didn't want to risk asking. A "no" from Mom was final.

He managed to get out the back door and onto his bike without anyone appearing in the back door or an upstairs window. The *other* person he didn't want to wake up was Fawn. She'd never let him get out of the shed with his bike, much less all the way to the ranch, without her. And if she went, he knew O. would stay hidden.

Fawn's gonna pound me if she ever finds out, Will thought.

But even that didn't keep him from riding furiously down Canyon Road and off to the south toward Mr. T.'s ranch. He didn't slow down until his fifteenth glance over his shoulder reassured him that Fawn wasn't behind him, ready to run him down.

Without the anxiety pulsing through him, Will could settle back on his bicycle seat and breathe the morning in. He wasn't the only one up and around at this early hour. Most of the adobe houses he passed as he left Santa Fe were already puffing out sweet-smelling piñon pine smoke, and some were even letting the aroma of cinnamon buns out through the cracks around their windows.

Above him the clouds were plume-shaped and still. Early morning was usually the only time New Mexico was motionless. The rest of the time, he could always count on a wind to stir things up. But in spite of moving air, it was almost always quiet, just as it was now—a brooding silence that had no sense of what

year it was or what was happening in the world. New Mexico just
wanted to be quiet.

Sometimes the silence was comforting to Will. It meant he
didn't have to answer to anyone when he was alone with it.

But at other times, it disturbed him. Those were the times
when he wanted to argue, wanted to convince the world that he
was right—and the silence of the never-ending mountains and
seamless sky wouldn't argue back.

Today was one of those times. That, he decided, was why he
wanted to talk to O. some more. She would let him speak his
piece—and she would speak hers—and maybe it would all make
sense.

The thought of it made him pedal faster, until he was puffing
like the chimney on Mr. T.'s hacienda when he arrived. The
smoke rising told Will somebody was up in the house, so he
walked his bike quickly past it and parked it on the other side of
the stables where it couldn't be seen out the kitchen window. He
felt a prick of guilt. As he slipped inside the stable and looked
back to make sure there was no one following him, it did seem
sneaky.

But that faded the minute Gabby spotted him and his big lips
grinned from his beanstalk height. His eyes were kind as he
looked down at Will, who leaned casually against a stall.

"Morning," Will said.

"You're up early, ain't ya?" Gabby said.

"I—uhh—thought a ride before it gets too hot might be
nice," Will said.

Gabby chuckled, and Will wanted to bite his tongue off. *Too
hot? It's March, stupid! You'll be lucky if it hits 50 degrees!* Right
now his hands were stiff with the cold, even punched inside his
pockets.

Gabby reached up and patted Cisco's nose. "He likes an early
ride," he said. "He won't be so anxious to come haulin' back

here, seein's how it won't be so close to feedin' time."

"Oh, it won't be close at all!" Will said. "I'll be back in maybe an hour."

Gabby nodded and once again gave Will a big-lipped grin. "I'll get you a saddle," he said, and loped off toward the tack room. Will sagged with relief—until Gabby stopped in the doorway and looked at him, a puzzled expression on his face.

"Where are your two sidekicks today?" he said.

Will felt himself seizing up. But he had to say something, or Gabby was going to suspect that all was not as it should be.

"They'll be along," Will said finally. That was true; he was sure they would be once they discovered he'd gone off without them.

Gabby nodded again, until Will was certain he saw his ears flap. "Yep," he said. "Sometimes a feller's just gotta get off by hisself."

"Yeah," Will said weakly. "That's it."

That really was it, partly, and Will felt that prick of guilt again, although this time it was more like a stab. It would be nice to just tell Gabby the truth.

As Gabby continued on into the tack room, Will almost called out and stopped him. But no sooner had he opened his mouth than he heard the back door slam up at the house. Will hurried to the stable door and, flattening himself against the wall, leaned around and peeked out. Mr. Tarantino was coming crisply down the steps, his eyes already on the stables. Will ducked out of the doorway and plastered himself to the wall again. He could practically see his heart pounding under his jacket. An argument started in his head.

He's gonna catch me trying to get out of here without asking permission to ride alone!

So what's the big deal? If you tell him you need some time alone, he'll understand.

But that's not the only reason I'm going. That would kind of be a lie.

So you'd rather sneak than lie—is that it?

I'd rather do neither, but I need this so bad. If I don't get away I'm gonna suffocate.

Even as he thought it, Will could barely breathe. He sucked in air and tried to find the words he would say once Mr. Tarantino darkened the stable doorway, waiting for an explanation.

And then, from the direction of the house, Will heard a man's voice call out, "Señor Tarantino! Telephone!"

The boot steps Will had heard coming toward him stopped and then started up again, fading in the other direction. If Will had sagged with relief before, he was ready to collapse now. He pushed himself away from the wall and dove for Cisco's stall, where Gabby was just cinching up the saddle.

"Thanks, Gabby," Will said. He tried not to sound like he was in too much of a hurry, though he was sure the way he hiked himself up on the stirrup before Gabby could even get out of the way was a dead giveaway.

"Have you a good ride," Gabby said. "And don't get heat stroke out there, now."

Will glanced quickly at him, but Gabby was grinning, his kind eyes twinkling.

"Yeah," Will said, and then he walked Cisco out of the stables and took off through the gate at a trot.

Okay, so now *I feel like a complete moron!* he thought as he put the ranch behind him in a cloud of Cisco's dust. If Gabby mentioned that to Mr. T., who was obviously going to appear in the stable once he finished his phone call, Mr. T. was going to see right through it and know Will had been making up an excuse.

When the ranch was well out of sight, Will slowed Cisco

down with a pull on the reins. *Maybe I oughta just turn back*, he thought. *Maybe this just isn't worth it. Maybe—*

But that possibility stopped abruptly on his lips as a figure popped up from behind a rock. The same rock where he'd last seen her.

"O.!" Will said.

"You were expecting maybe Pancho Villa?" she said. The mane of dark hair was tied up in a bun on top of her head today and fastened in place with string. Will couldn't help staring at it. Even Fawn, who couldn't have cared less about her appearance, wouldn't have worn a string in her hair. Mom wouldn't let her, for one thing.

"Isn't it still considered rude out there in civilization to stare?" O. said.

Will shook himself back to the present and pulled his eyes away from O.'s hairdo.

"Yeah," he said. "But I'm a smart aleck, remember?"

"No, you're a smart Will. That's your name, right?"

"Yeah," Will said. The fact that she remembered it made his cheeks feel like they were turning the shade of a turkey's neck. He felt about as awkward as a turkey at the moment, so it probably worked.

But he didn't want it working for long. He jerked his head. "You wanna go for a ride?" he said.

O. shot up a dark eyebrow. "With you? On that horse? Uh, no—not the way you ride."

"What's wrong with the way I ride?"

"If you'll recall, you almost ran over me with that same horse. That didn't exactly instill confidence in me."

Will wasn't sure what "instill" meant, but he didn't want to appear even more stupid in front of this girl, so he just shrugged and let himself down off of Cisco's back.

"So why'd you want me to come back today?" he said.

"I'm bored and you're pretty much the most interesting thing I've come across in a while, so I figured I'd let you entertain me 'til I got bored again."

"Who do I look like, Mickey Rooney?"

O. frowned as Will crossed in front of her and climbed up onto the rock. "Who?" she said.

Will gave her a long look. "Mickey Rooney. You know, the movie star that's in all those Andy Hardy movies. Andy Hardy's *Blonde Trouble*, Andy Hardy's *Double Life,* Andy—"

"Never heard of him," O. said, and deftly pulled herself up onto the rock beside him.

"How long have you been living out here?" Will said, eyes bugging, he was sure. "Everybody's heard of Andy Hardy."

"I don't live here, remember? I don't live anywhere. You know nothing about me."

"Wanna bet? I know you're a girl."

"Amazing," she said, her voice dry. "You're a genius."

"And I know you're about 12, like me."

"Thirteen," she said. Then she made a face, as if she wanted to kick herself for letting that out.

"Gotcha," Will said.

"You did not 'get me.' " She shook her head. "No more questions from you. I'll do the asking."

"Pretty bossy, aren't you?" Will said.

"Yeah," she said, "so get used to it."

Before Will could protest, O. began to pepper him with questions. The answers all involved things he liked to talk about— needed to talk about—and so he opened up like a barn door and let it all out.

"I want to know what's going on with the war," she said. "Are we winning?"

Then it was, "What's junior high like? I never got to go." And then, "Is the Depression over?"

The more she asked, the more Will was sure she hadn't seen a newspaper or heard a radio for at least three years. She soaked up everything he said as if she were a dried-out sponge.

But although a lot of what he told her obviously surprised her—because her dark eyes opened wide or her eyebrows arched up or she craned her neck out toward him—she never said anything like, "Jeepers creepers!" or "You're jiving me!" Those expressions had been around since before the war started, and she couldn't have been gone *that* long. She at least knew there *was* a war. It was as if she were almost an adult, even though she was only a year older than Will himself. Although Will began to feel less like a long-legged turkey around her, he felt like he had to stay on his toes. He hated to admit it, but it was possible she was smarter than he was.

When she started asking about what clothes styles were now fashionable, Will found himself getting a little restless. It was time to take the upper hand.

"Come on," he said. "Let's just go for a ride on my horse. We'll make it short." He nudged her with his elbow. "You know you want to."

O. rolled her eyes, but Will also saw her steal a wistful glance at Cisco, who was waiting patiently in the shade.

"All right," O. said. "But don't get impetuous on me."

"I can't," Will said. "I don't even know what that is."

"Good," she said. "Then I'm still at least one step ahead of you."

Will grunted and climbed into the saddle. He put a hand down to pull O. up, but she pushed it away and managed to mount Cisco herself, landing neatly behind Will.

Isn't there anything she doesn't know or can't do? Will thought. Except for being about three years behind the times, she was definitely outdoing him.

But instead of making him grumpy, the thought actually

gave him a shot of energy, as if he'd just discovered something new. He wasn't sure what it was yet, but it didn't matter. He knocked his heels into Cisco's sides and said, "Hold on, O.!"

"You said you'd go slow!" she cried out behind him.

"Depends on your idea of slow!" Will shouted back and then urged Cisco on.

Cisco had obviously been waiting for just such a challenge all his horse life, because he lowered his head and took off down the trail, leaving Will breathless as he encouraged him to go even faster.

"No!" O. shouted. But there was laughter in her voice, and Will could feel her hair whipping around, giving him the occasional slap on the back of the neck. *So much for the string,* he thought.

"Don't you dare make me fall off this horse!" she laughed into the wind.

"Then hold on," Will said, " 'cause you ain't seen nothin' yet!"

As O. wrapped both arms around Will's middle, he wasn't exactly sure what he was going to show her next. As it turned out, there was no time to even think of it. From out of the corner of his eye, Will caught movement off to the left. Before he could even register that it was a jackrabbit, headed right for them, Cisco let out a whinny Will could feel in the horse's belly with his legs.

"It's okay, Cisco!" Will started to say. But Cisco didn't agree. Suddenly he threw himself up on his back legs, his front hooves coming straight off the ground. Will clung to the saddle horn, but with a jerk, O.'s arms came loose from around him. Even as Will whipped around to grab her, she slid straight to the ground and landed heavily, right on her back.

✢ ✢ ✢

Chapter Eleven

*C*isco seemed to know that he'd made a mistake. He brought his front hooves down and danced to a stop, his head hanging and the whites of his eyes showing.

Will barely gave him a second look as he scrambled off his back and crouched down beside O. Her eyes were closed, and her face was as pale as paper. Will's mouth went dry.

"Hey," he whispered, "are you all right?"

"I will be," she said, without opening her eyes. "As long as you don't talk any louder than that."

"Okay," Will whispered. He rubbed his hands helplessly up and down on the front of his pant legs. "Can you move?"

"I don't want to move," she said. She shook her head and winced as if Will had punched her.

"I gotta go get help," Will said.

He started to get up, but she snatched at his jacket sleeve, her eyes wide open.

"I'll be fine in a minute," she said. "No help."

"I could just get Mr. T. He wouldn't tell anybody—"

"No!" Before the word was even out, she drew up her face and clenched her fingers around Will's sleeve.

"Don't talk," he said.

"Then don't say stupid things." O. opened her eyes again and looked at him. "Just give me a minute and I'll be able to get up. It just knocked the wind out of me."

"Should I be doing something?" Will said.

"You should be making a vow never to ride a horse again. You're dangerous."

She half smiled, half shivered. Will yanked his jacket off and put it over her, tucking it up under chin.

"You have great bedside manner," she said. "You should be a doctor. Be anything but a cowboy."

O. gave a forced laugh. Will had never felt less like laughing. He had to put his hand over his mouth to keep from blurting out anything stupid and possibly ending up bawling in front of her.

This is all my fault, he would have said. *I could have killed you. What if you do die? I'm an idiot. I'm a moron!*

"Okay," O. said. "I'm gonna try to sit up. Don't let me fall down if I don't make it all the way, all right?"

"Yeah," Will said. "You want me to pull you up?"

"No. I can do it."

Gritting her teeth, O. rolled to one side and got up on an elbow. She closed her eyes, but not before Will saw the tears coming. Slowly she got to a sitting position, with Will holding an arm behind her in case she flopped back down to the ground.

She sat there breathing hard for a minute and then she said, "All right, I'm going to try to stand up, but I'm going to have to lean on you."

"Sure," Will said. He crawled closer and got his shoulder under her arm. She put it around him and together they stood up. She gave a yelp that out-whimpered Abe and leaned against him like a falling tree. Will held on with everything he had. If he let her fall, he knew he would be the one to die—of embarrassment.

"Just walk me a few steps so I can see if I can do it," she said.

"Are you nuts?" Will said. "You can't try to walk; you just got thrown off a horse!"

"I can do anything I want, all right? Let's get that straight right now."

"You *are* nuts," Will said.

He could feel his own knees shaking as O. took a tentative step forward with him at her side, holding her up, so he could imagine how hers must feel. Even as he thought it, she buckled and would have gone down if Will hadn't held on.

"I just need a little more time," she said.

Will wasn't so sure about that. It might have been his own fear playing tricks on him, but he was fairly certain her voice was getting weaker, and she was starting to breathe like a little puppy.

"Why don't I just put you up on Cisco and take you home?"

"What is it about the word no—is it a foreign language to you?"

"Enough with the I-don't-have-a-home business," Will said. "You have to live somewhere and you're hurt and I need to take you there."

"No," she said through her teeth. "It would mean big trouble if you went to my—where I live."

"I have parents!" Will said. "I know how mad they get when you get hurt because you were fooling around. And I was the one fooling around so I should be the one—"

"So you're a knight in shining armor," O. said. "But you'd have to be Lancelot himself to make my father understand." She bit her lip. "Look—all right, you can take me almost home and then you have to let me off and I'll make it the rest of the way.

But you can't come in—you can't even come near. I just don't want my father seeing that somebody knows where we live." She glared at him. "And if you ask me why, I'll rip your lips off."

Will didn't like it, but it was better than watching her crawl her way across the desert. *Besides,* he thought, *maybe by the time we get there, she'll change her mind.*

After all, it had to be quite a distance to any place she might live. There were no houses around here; he and Fawn and Miguel knew that for sure.

O. was watching him carefully, and for a second Will was sure she'd read his thoughts. He shrugged.

"It's a deal," he said. "Only—you can't climb up on Cisco by yourself. You're gonna have to let me help you."

She glared at him again. "You're liking this, aren't you? You're just loving the fact that I can't keep up with you now."

"You're nuts," Will said.

"Oh, but I'm still smarter than you are."

"Really?" Will said. He helped her lift her foot up to the stirrup and guided her as she dragged her leg to Cisco's other side. The horse nickered and sidestepped, but Will murmured to him until he settled down again.

"What do you mean 'really'?" O. said when she was in the saddle.

"I mean, if you're so smart, then how come you're going to ride with me again?"

"Nice try," she said. "But you're walking, and I'm riding."

It was, of course, the only way to do it—Will leading Cisco by the reins while O. tried to hang onto the saddle horn.

Will kept a tight hold on Cisco, forcing him to pick his way slowly over clumps of grass and around junipers. Even at that, O. let out the occasional moan. Each time, Will ordered Cisco to stop, but O. informed Will she wasn't a sissy and would he just get on with it.

She directed Will up to the crest of a hill not far from where Will had fallen into the turquoise mine. As soon as they reached the top, O. began to wriggle her way from Cisco's back.

"What are you doing?" Will said.

"I'm getting off."

"Where's your house?"

O. glared at him. "I told you I'm going to go the last little bit by myself."

Gathering up her face as if to keep from crying out, O. slid down from Cisco's back and touched her feet to the dirt. Her knees gave, and Will caught her clumsily before she crumpled to the ground.

"I wasn't going to fall," she said. But she didn't immediately pull away. She sagged against Will for a brief moment, and Will almost took that opportunity to pick her up and set her back up on Cisco's back. But she was too fast for him and got herself upright on her own and stood there, wobbly but determined.

"How far do you have to go?" Will asked.

"Don't think you're going to trick me," O. said. "And I'm not going anywhere until I'm sure you're far away from here, so get going."

"But—"

"Go. So help me, I'll give this horse a swat that will set him off running, and then *you'll* be the one who has to walk all the way home."

"Yeah, but what if you can't make it?"

"I told you, I'm—"

But before she could finish her sentence, a male voice cracked in the air like the snapping of a whip. "Olive!" it yelled.

O. looked at Will. "Now he's mad at me," she whispered. "Wonderful."

She gave Will a shove toward Cisco.

"Go!" she whispered. "Walk your horse to the bottom of the hill and then ride out of here."

"Olive!"

"I'm coming, Daddy!"

O.—who Will knew by now was the Olive the angry voice was calling to—turned once more to Will. "Go," she said. "Or you're really going to make trouble for me. As much as you seem to love to do that—just don't this time, okay?"

Will opened his mouth to argue with her. She was getting paler and weaker by the minute—she looked as if she could barely stand up, much less walk to face the man who was obviously ready to chew her out. He couldn't just leave her here.

But the man yelled out her name again, this time accompanied by a series of words Will had never heard before, but which he was pretty sure a kid his age wasn't supposed to hear. Olive didn't say anything, but gave him one more shove. It was barely enough to make him lean, but he did what she said. In fact, as he grabbed Cisco's reins, he had to force himself not to run the horse down the hill. But the voice Olive used to cry out, "I'm coming, Daddy!" had some of that fear etched into it—the fear he'd seen ripple through her eyes before. Somehow he knew that little bit of fear would be so much bigger if her father knew Will had ever been there.

So moving as stealthily as a thief, Will led Cisco down the hill at a silent walk. Above, he could hear Olive descending the hill on the other side, her voice fading with each cry of, "I'm here, Daddy! I'll be right there," until he could no longer hear her.

When Will reached the bottom, he stopped for a minute and strained his ears for sounds, but there was only the faint rise and fall of voices. No one charged up the other side of the hill after him. And at least Olive was no longer alone with her injuries.

Still, as Will mounted Cisco and dug his heels in for the ride home, he couldn't help but wonder what would happen to her when her father got her home—wherever that was.

I shoulda taken her all the way to her house anyway, no matter what she said, Will thought miserably. *I chickened out. I let her dad scare me—and he can't be that bad. Olive's an all right person, so her father couldn't be as mean as he sounded.*

All the way back to the ranch, Will tried to convince himself that Olive's father had only been upset because he couldn't find her, because she'd been gone longer than she'd said she'd be.

Mom gets mad at me when I get home late.

But not that mad. Not mad enough to swear at him and sound like she wanted to string him up by his thumbs.

I shoulda taken her all the way home and explained to him that it was my fault she got hurt, and then I shoulda stayed there until I was sure he wasn't gonna clobber her or somethin'.

As he rode through the gate and on to the stable, Will was so busy beating himself up in his mind, he didn't see Mr. T. standing in the stable doorway until he climbed down from Cisco's back to lead him inside. Gabby slipped out of nowhere and took the reins, and Mr. T. looked down at Will with an expression Will couldn't put a name to.

"I need to have a word with you, Son," he said.

It had to be anger.

"I have to unsaddle Cisco and wipe him down and—"

"Gabby will do it. Let's go."

Or maybe disappointment.

"Did I do something wrong?" Will said.

Mr. T. closed his eyes and put a hand on the back of Will's neck. It was cold and clammy, the way Will's got when he had to go to the dentist.

"Don't you ever—ever—go off alone like that again," Mr. T. said. "Do you understand me?"

Will nodded. And then he knew what the expression was. It was fear.

Mr. T. nodded his head toward the house. "Let's go inside," he said.

"I'm sorry, sir," Will said as he followed him, nearly running to keep up with Mr. T.'s long strides. "I didn't know you didn't want us to ride by ourselves, honest. And please don't take away Fawn and Miguel's riding privileges—they didn't know about it—it was just me."

Mr. T. didn't answer. He just led the way to the house and nodded for Will to go inside. The spicy smell of preparations for *huevos rancheros*—the Spanish-style eggs Will usually drooled over—was everywhere, but Will was far from hungry as he trailed Mr. T. into the big tiled kitchen and took the chair he pointed to. He would, in fact, rather have eaten the bottom of his boot than to sit at the table with Mr. T. and hear more of his disappointment.

Mr. T. went to the stove and left Will in agony while he cooked. It gave Will time to work up a good case of nausea, so that when Mr. T. slid the eggs onto two plates and put them both on the table, Will thought he would choke.

"Eat," Mr. T. said as he took his place across from Will. "And let's talk."

Afraid now to tell Mr. T. he already felt like he had his entire boot in his throat, Will cut obediently into his eggs and felt the salsa burn his tongue.

"I can see I'm going to have to set some clearer rules," Mr. T. said. "Son, I just can't have you kids going off alone on the horses. The desert can be dangerous."

Yeah, no kidding, Will thought. The sound of Olive's father yelling at her still echoed in his head. But the words that bounced back to him from the walls of his mind weren't Olive's father's, but his own: *I got her in so much trouble, I'm probably never gonna see her again.*

But he had to. He had to at least make sure she was all right—and tell her he was sorry. And the only way to do that was to ride Cisco. For that reason alone, he riveted his attention on Mr. T., who had produced a piece of paper from somewhere and, pushing his breakfast aside, drew a square in the center of it.

"Every rule I write in this box," Mr. T. said, "is not open for discussion. It is final and there will be no argument about it." He looked up at Will, his eyes squinted more tightly than Will had ever seen them. "If you or Fawn or Miguel break any of these rules, you will no longer be allowed to ride the horses. Am I clear?"

Will nodded. His heart was pounding.

"Any topic we write outside the box," Mr. T. said, running a finger around the outskirts of the square, "is open for discussion."

Then put riding alone outside the box, Will wanted to say, *because I have to go out there by myself one more time. Please!*

But even as he watched, the egg growing cold in his mouth, Mr. T. printed "No riding alone" squarely in the middle of the box.

He also added "No riding after dark" and "No going after suspected cattle rustlers."

Will swallowed hard and poked a finger at the space outside the box. "So what's left to go here?" he said.

"What would you like to go there?" Mr. T. said. "Bring it up and I'll tell you where it goes."

Will shrugged. He really didn't feel like discussing it. Just the fact that there were some things he wouldn't even be able to give his opinion on and argue for made him want to tear the paper into shreds.

"Well?" Mr. T. said.

But Will was spared from having to answer by a rap on the back door.

"Come in," Mr. T. said, not taking his eyes off of Will.

"Hey, Mr. T.," said Fawn before she even had the door open all the way, "have you seen—"

She stopped so abruptly when she saw Will, Miguel nearly walked up the back of her legs. Both of them stood in the doorway, looking at Will. Fawn was obviously madder than the proverbial wet hen, and even Miguel looked disappointed at the very least. It made Will squirm in his chair. He looked down and poked at his eggs with his fork until the salsa mixed with the egg yolk and made a bloody-looking mess on his plate.

"You already went riding without us," Fawn said as she stomped across the room.

"Yeah," Will said. "So?"

"So—what gives?" she said. "That's not fair!"

"Are you mad at us, Will?" Miguel said in his quiet voice.

Why doesn't anybody get it? Will wanted to scream. *I'm not mad at you! I'm mad at everything that's keeping me from doing something—anything—so I won't go nuts!*

"You better not ever do that again, Will Hutchinson!" Fawn said.

"Don't worry, Fawn," Mr. T. said. "There will be no more solo riding by anybody. Come on over here and let me show you something."

Fawn and Miguel hurried to the table to get an explanation of the "box." Will got up and scraped his dish into the waste can. With each swipe of the fork, he tried to push away the anger that was building up inside.

But it didn't work.

✝ ⸎ ✝

Chapter Twelve

O ver the next couple of weeks, nothing could turn down the
heat on Will's anger. Instead, it built up, stronger and
stronger, like water boiling in a pot with the lid on it.

Every day he and Miguel and Fawn went riding, and every
day Will grew more resentful because he couldn't look for Olive
on his own. To make matters worse, he never saw her when they
were out digging for turquoise in the black tailings or sketching
pictures of the mine shaft for their model or even when they
were sitting and snacking atop the hill where he'd last seen her.
He was sure that she was hurt worse than he'd thought, or that
her angry father wouldn't let her even leave the house.

After a while, Will refused to eat any of the snacks Señora
Otero packed for them. They all turned to sawdust in his mouth
anyway.

"Why does this bag come back still half full every day?" she
asked one afternoon when the kids returned from their ride and
were washing their hands in the kitchen where she was prepar-
ing supper for Mr. T.

"Because Will doesn't eat," Fawn said. "I don't think he likes your cooking anymore."

"I do so!" Will said, his cheeks immediately going scarlet. Sometimes, it was all he could do not to bean Fawn right on the head.

"Liar," Fawn said. "Every day we say, 'Will, you want some?' and every day he says no."

Miguel looked anxiously from Will to Fawn. "I do not think that is because he does not like my mother's food," he said. "I think he is only not so hungry."

"Yeah," Will said. "That's it."

"We better call the doctor, then," Fawn said with a decisive nod. "Because if he's not hungry, he's sick."

"I am *not!*" Will said.

He turned from the sink and flicked a fingerful of soapy water at her.

She let out a screech that probably had the horses whinnying out in the stables. Miguel watched as if he were in pain.

"All right, *mi hija*," Señora Otero said to Fawn, "I think it is time for all young ladies to mind their manners."

"What about *his* manners?" Fawn said, jabbing a finger in Will's direction.

Señora Otero ignored that and said in her soft voice, "Why don't you take some apples out to the horses? They will love you forever."

Fawn gave Will one long, sour look before she gave in and collected three apples. Miguel followed her out the door; Will was sure the Señora had given him a mother-signal to do that.

"You are troubled, my friend," she said to Will when Fawn and Miguel were gone. "Can I help in some way?"

Will wanted to open his mouth and let it all belch out of him—his worry over Olive and his frustration at not being able to go and find her again. It was all becoming painful to hold inside him. And if anyone would show him some understanding, it would be Señora Otero.

"You know you can speak with me anytime," she went on as she returned to the counter where she eased out dough on a board with her hands. "I will be here every day when you children come. I am Señor Tarantino's cook and housekeeper now."

Will looked at her, startled. "You are?" he said.

"Yes. I can no longer expect Uncle José to support us in his house with the meager amount he makes selling his santos."

"So—that means Mr. T.'s your boss?"

She smiled down at the dough. "Yes, I suppose he is."

Terrific, Will thought. He could feel his shoulders slumping. That meant she wouldn't argue with Mr. T. for him to take that one rule out of the box. So what was the point in telling her anything?

"I'm fine," he said. And the anger bubbled even harder inside him.

One day in the school cafeteria, as Will was poking his finger into his peanut butter sandwich over and over, just to keep from poking somebody in the eye, he noticed Neddie watching him curiously.

"What?" Will said, the irritation climbing up the back of his neck.

"That looks like somebody shot it full of bullet holes," Neddie said.

Will blinked at the sandwich.

"It does," Neddie said. "Or maybe it's a wall some termites ate up. Giant termites. Man-eating termites!"

Neddie's eyes were alive behind his glasses. *He can dream up just about anything,* Will thought. *I wonder if he could help me think of a way—*

Will looked around for Miguel, who was still going through the lunch line, and leaned across the table. "So, Neddie," he said, in a low voice. "What if you met somebody out in the desert and you saw this person get hurt and you wanted to go back and check on the person only nobody would let you and you couldn't tell them about the person? What would you do?"

For a moment, Neddie looked a little baffled, but his imagination seemed to quickly overcome that, and his eyes took on a fiendish shine.

"Well," he said, rubbing his hands together, "you could sneak out in the dead of the night, all dressed in black."

Will nodded. "Yeah. Go on."

"You could slither along on the floor of the desert like a snake—with only the moonlight to guide you—only you would have to be careful that you didn't meet up with an actual snake, or a coyote, or a Gila monster—I hear those are really poisonous—"

"Okay, so forget the animals. I'm—I mean, the *person*—is crawling around like a snake. Then what?"

Neddie's eyes grew a little vague. "Then—you would—hide in a cave until daylight, and then you would have to get out of there because of bats, which I understand will hide in your hair, thinking it's a nest—and then you—"

"Never mind," Will said, waving him off. Miguel was approaching the table, and besides, Neddie was no help. He was making the whole thing seem more impossible than ever.

And the more out of reach it seemed, the more ready Will was to punch out some headlights or snatch somebody bald-headed. With Mr. T. always watching him, Will knew better than to show any of his anger at school or at the ranch, so he concentrated on the New Mexico Treasures project. Although Fawn complained endlessly about being bored, Will and Miguel dragged her with them every day out to the old turquoise tailings to dig for even a tiny piece of the blue-green stone. They had everything else done—the model of the mine shaft and the outcropping-hill made with modeling clay and real dirt specimens they carried home with them, as well as their written report and their plan for the oral presentation. The one thing Will thought about almost as much as he did about finding Olive was winning the contest. Right then, it was the only battle he had any hope of winning.

"I'm sick of doing this!" Fawn whined one day when they'd been digging for almost an hour. "Will, I promise I'll do your dishes for a week if you won't make me do this one more minute."

"You don't have to do it," Will said.

"Huh? If I don't do it, I'll feel like a lazy bum, sitting around while you two do all the work." She scowled. "I just wish we'd find a piece of stupid turquoise so we can do something fun."

"What would you like to do, Fawn?" Miguel said.

Will grunted. He was pretty sure Miguel didn't care what Fawn wanted to do. He was just trying to shut her up so Will wouldn't pop her one.

As Miguel listened to Fawn rattle on about the adventures she would much rather be having, Will watched him out of the corner of his eye.

He really is my friend, Will thought. *I bet I could tell him and he'd help me.* Mentally he shook his head. *I couldn't tell Fawn. She wouldn't just help me find Olive and then back off. She'd have to be right in there, and then Olive would be mad at me.*

And not only that, but he was sure her father would scream and do heaven knew what else.

But Miguel—he wouldn't even ask any questions. He'd just do whatever Will asked him to and then fade away.

Will felt a pang of guilt. *Why didn't I think of this sooner?* he thought. *How come I didn't trust him?*

That wasn't hard to answer. As they gave up on finding any

turquoise for the day and climbed back on the horses for the ride back to the ranch, Will hung back, his thoughts heavy in his head. *It's because I can't talk to* any*body,* he thought. *Mom just doesn't want me to upset anyone. Mr. T. wants me to choose my battles, but this one is in the box so I* have *no choice. Reverend Bud isn't even here.*

By the time they got back to the ranch, Will was feeling so down it was an effort to dismount and lead Cisco to his stall for his grooming and his supper. Fawn was already finished and had danced off to the house when Will was still pouring oats into a bucket. Miguel climbed up onto the stall door and swung back and forth as he waited for him.

Will looked around to be sure no one, not even Gabby, was within earshot. This was the perfect chance to talk to Miguel, and if he didn't grab it, there might not be another one.

"Uh, Miguel," he said. He emptied the last of the oats into Cisco's bucket and stroked the horse's mane as he began to chomp.

"Yes, my friend?"

Will cringed. Somehow, that made it harder.

Miguel was still watching him closely.

"Uh—I have kind of a favor to ask you."

"Anything."

Stop being so nice! Will wanted to shout. *I've been a lousy friend! You're making me feel guilty.*

"Is it about Fawn?" Miguel said.

Will looked at him. "Huh?" he said.

"Fawn—how do you say it—gets on your nerve."

"My nerves—plural. All of them!" Will said.

"I try to help, because I know you are troubled by her."

"By Fawn?" Will said. "No—it's not her. It's—"

"Hello, out here!"

Will jumped, nearly knocking the bucket out from under

Cisco's nose. The horse whinnied slightly and went on chewing.

"Mom?" Will said. He could feel his face going crimson. There was no way she could have known what he was about to say to Miguel, but he felt as if he had just been caught with his entire arm in the cookie jar. What was she doing here?

"Where are you?" she sang out. He heard her chuckle and say to someone, "Why they would rather smell this than your cooking is beyond me."

Will knew his face was turning another shade deeper. His mother was with Señora Otero.

When they both appeared in the stall doorway, which Miguel swung open for them, Miguel jumped down and went to his mother, who kissed him on the forehead and ran her hand over his hair.

I'd run like the dickens if Mom did that to me in front of my friends, Will thought.

Mom, of course, wouldn't. And Miguel didn't seem to mind at all that *his* mother did. He looked at Señora Otero as if at that moment she were the most important person on earth, and she looked back the same way.

Suddenly, Will shivered.

He couldn't ask Miguel to do something behind his mother's back.

"Supper is ready," Señora Otero said. "Unless you boys would like some more time. You were having a serious conversation?"

"Yes, we were—"

"No, we weren't!"

Both mothers looked at their sons. Will shook his head firmly. "We were done talking. I'll be up in a minute. I just have to get some fresh hay."

Señora Otero looked a little disappointed. She put her arm around Miguel and headed for the stable door, looking back over her shoulder at Will's mom.

"I'll wait for Will," Mom said. "We'll be up before the tamales get cold."

Will scurried out of the stall and headed for the loft. The last thing he wanted to do was be alone with his mother. She had a way of reading his mind just by looking at his face, and he wasn't sure what his face was saying right now. It was as if he was losing control of everything.

But Mom followed him, right up to the hayloft, and took the pitchfork out of Will's hand the moment he picked it up.

"Sit down, Son," she said.

"Mom, I gotta—"

"What you 'gotta' do is sit," she said.

Will sank uneasily into the hay. She sat across from him and got right to the point.

"Word came out today that Iwo Jima has finally been secured by the Allies."

"You mean, we beat the Japanese there?" Will said.

Mom nodded. "There is a breathtaking photograph on the front page of the newspaper taken about a month ago—soldiers planting the American flag on—oh, what is that place called? Mt. something—Suribachi? Is that it? Anyway, it's 550 feet high—where all the world can see it."

Will could hear his heart in his ears. "That means only one more to go," he said. "Just Okinawa and we've got 'em."

"The radio said we took out 22,000 Japanese soldiers," she said. "The war could be over in a few months, Will."

For the first time, Will realized that his mother was close to tears, and that was something that almost never happened. It made his own throat feel tight.

"Are you okay, Mom?" he said.

"I am," she said. "And then again, I'm not." She looked at him, close and deep. "Son, you have done so well through all this, and you've grown so much. I know it's been hard, and it will continue to be hard until the end. But we have such a short time to go, compared with how long we have already waited. Please try not to let your anger get the best of you now."

Will could only stare at her. He'd thought he'd been hiding it so well. How had she known?

"You can't help how you feel," she went on. "I of all people know that. Even God doesn't expect you not to have any bad feelings. But it's what you do with them that counts. Not only can you hurt yourself, but you can hurt other people without even knowing it."

Will was too confused to argue with her. He had no idea what she was talking about.

"I don't think you've noticed it," she said, "but Abe has been acting strangely lately."

"He has?" Will said.

Mom's mouth twitched. "Like I said, I don't think you've noticed it. He's been unusually quiet and I've seen him chewing on his fist more than usual."

Will felt as if guilt had grabbed him and was squeezing the breath out of him. "You want me to talk to him? I've been so busy with this social studies project and stuff I haven't taken much time with him, but I think he'll listen to me—"

"He certainly does listen to you," Mom said. "I finally got it out of him this afternoon that he thinks he's stupid because he's afraid of the horses. Somehow, he got that idea from you."

"I didn't tell him that!" Will cried. "I tried to explain it to him, Mom—you gotta believe me!"

"Oh, I do. But you know Abe has trouble understanding things. I don't think it has quite sunk in."

"I'll talk to him again!"

"You can do that," Mom said, "but I think actions speak louder than words."

Will felt himself squinting at her, the way Mr. T. did. "What do you want me to do?"

"Now that your report is almost done—"

"How'd you know that?"

"Fawn told me."

"Since when did she get to be such a blabbermouth?" Will said.

"Since she turned 11 and started to become an almost-teenager instead of a little girl. She needs some female companionship, and since you and Miguel are both boys, she comes to me." Mom actually smiled this time. "Don't tell her anything you don't want me to know."

Will suddenly felt as if every escape route were somehow closing off and he was being trapped in his anger with no way out.

"Anyway," Mom was saying, "since you aren't on a mission out there with the horses anymore, maybe you could take Abe with you, just a little way at first, and try to get him used to the horses, help him get some confidence. That's why I brought him out here with me tonight—so maybe he could just come out here with you and visit with them."

The last exit slammed shut. Will didn't know whether to cry or pick up the pitchfork and hurl it out the barn window. Now there never *would* be a chance to find Olive. It was hopeless.

There was absolutely no battle he could win.

☩ ☩ ☩

Chapter Thirteen

*A*s the next few weeks passed, Will was sure that the box
Mr. T. had drawn for him was now filling up the entire
paper. It might as well, he thought, because there was nothing
outside the box he really *wanted* to try to negotiate.

The biggest item outside the rule-square was Abe, and Will
went at spending time with him like a new career. Every afternoon, as soon as Abe got home from the Opportunity School,
Mom brought him out to the ranch. Miguel, Fawn, and Will
timed their rides so that they would be back in the barn when
Abe arrived so he could "help" Will feed and groom Cisco.

Actually, he wasn't a lot of help. He still spent most of his
time cowering in the corner of the stall, eyes wide and mouth
even wider. After the first week, Will was finally able to convince
him that Cisco did not bite the hand that fed him, and Abe
poured the oats into Cisco's bucket, keeping a wary eye to make
sure Will was holding the horse's head. When Abe saw Cisco
begin to chomp, however, it was as if someone had given Abe
himself a treat. He jumped up and down and clapped until Will

was certain the stables were going to come down.

It was good to see his big friend happy, and it helped ease *some* of the anger in Will. Even his mother noticed it and complimented him when Will came to her to do the good-night pinky-finger linking one evening.

"It's nothin'," Will told her.

"It is far from nothing," Mom said. "God smiles on unselfish acts."

Will grunted, and Mom's eyebrows shot up. She put down the copy of *TIME* magazine she was reading—the one with the picture on the cover of the soldiers planting the flag on Mt. Suribachi, which was now everywhere—and said, "What does that mean—that grunt?"

"I'm thinking, if God smiled on unselfish acts, Dad would be home instead of—where he is."

"Are you having some God-doubts, Son?" she asked.

Even as Will was automatically shaking his head, something struck him: He hadn't thought very much about God at all for, well, for a long time.

"I guess I'm mad at God," he said.

"That's obvious," Mom said dryly. "Have you told *Him* that?"

Will shook his head. "I figure He already knows. Doesn't He know everything?"

"He does, but He likes to hear it from the horse's mouth, as it were."

"Why?" Will said.

"Because it does *you* good to get your anger out, and who better to do it with than God?"

"Somebody who answers, for openers."

It was Mom's turn to grunt. "You cannot tell me you think God hasn't answered our prayers over and over during this war."

Will shrugged, but Mom gave him a hard look.

"Okay, yeah, He has," Will said.

"I hear a 'but' in there someplace," Mom said.

"You're not gonna get mad and send me to my room?" Will said.

"You can say anything you want to me, son—as long as you aren't disrespectful."

"So this is outside the box," Will said.

She looked puzzled. Will filled her in on Mr. T.'s box idea.

"I have more respect for that man all the time," Mom said. "Okay, yes, this is outside the box. I can't force your relationship with God."

That took Will by surprise, and he found himself staring at his mother.

"What?" she said.

"You mean I don't *have* to believe in turn-the-other-cheek?"

"I didn't say that. I said I can't *force* you to believe anything." Her mouth twitched. "However, God has His own box, and certain things in it are not open for discussion. He chooses His battles, just like the rest of us."

"I don't get that," Will said.

"Get me a piece of paper and I'll show you," Mom said.

Will produced paper and pencil, and Mom drew a square. "Is that the way Mr. T. did it?" she said.

Will nodded.

"Now, remember that I am doing this entirely off the cuff, and I could probably do a better job of it if I had some time to think about it, but right off the top of my head, the things that are in the box are—let's see—the Ten Commandments; the Two Great Commandments: You will love the Lord your God with everything that's in you and you'll love your neighbor as yourself; and—"

"Is turning the other cheek in the box?" Will said.

Mom nodded. "Jesus said it, so it must be in there."

"Oh," Will said.

"Exactly whose cheek is it that you want so badly to smack?" Mom said.

"Everybody's!"

Mom put the pencil down and sat back, arms folded. Her eyes were bright on Will. "Give me some names," she said.

Will didn't even think twice. The anger was already seeping out—she'd already seen it. There was no point in holding back now.

"Every Japanese that's holding Dad prisoner and killing our guys over there in the Pacific. I'd like to—"

"I get the idea," Mom said quickly. "Go on."

"And every German that's got Abe's parents and that's shooting at Fawn's father and every other American that's over there—in this whole stinkin' war."

"Keep going."

"And all the stupid people that say they're tired of supporting the war and are giving up—like that Percy Pants down at Hinkle's—"

"Uh-huh."

"And Mr. T. because he won't let me ride by myself—"

Mom's brow furrowed. "What's that all about?"

Will chomped down on his lip like Cisco biting into a mouthful of oats. He hadn't meant to blurt that out. It had just made its entrance along with everything else.

"I don't know," he said. He tried to say *I just want to spend some time by myself* or *It makes me think he doesn't trust me*—but those would have been lies. He couldn't lie to the face that was looking at him, obviously trying so hard to understand what was going on in his head.

"I can't change Mr. T.'s rules," she said finally. "But I can tell you this: that box gets smaller as you get older. Not God's box—that's the same for everybody. I mean the authority box, like Mr. T's. As you grow more mature, you can make more and more choices for yourself. You rely less and less on other people's boxes to guide you and more and more on God's. That's why it's so important for you to learn what's in God's box now so you can start making that transition." Mom actually smiled. "For off the top of my head, I'm doing pretty good!"

Will just nodded absently. He was slowly chewing on it all. Mom waited.

"But turn the other cheek never goes away," he said.

She tapped a finger on the table for a minute before she said, "The problem with focusing on just one verse is that you don't get the whole message. You have to study the *whole* Gospel to understand what it all means. You remember the story of Jesus overturning the tables in the temple?"

"Yeah," Will said. It had always been one of his personal favorites.

"He tore that place apart," Mom said. "Not because the people who were selling things at ridiculous prices right there in the temple were hurting *Him*—they were hurting *God* and God's people. That's how you decide which battles to fight."

Will's face lit up as if someone had suddenly flipped on a light switch in his head. Mom nodded.

"I love it when someone finally gets it," she said. "That must be why I love being a teacher. And when it happens to my son—"

"Okay, so if somebody's doing something to hurt somebody else, that hurts God, and you need to step in."

"If you can, yes," Mom said.

That was a pretty big "if." Although Will felt a little better after that conversation, it also made him more frustrated than ever. He was right to want to make sure Olive was okay—but he still couldn't figure out how he was supposed to do that and still stay in Mr. T.'s box.

As he lay in bed that night, listening to Abe snoring softly from across the room, Will went over the possibilities again, but every one was blocked by the rule: no riding alone. Even if he and Fawn and Miguel set out together and Will got away from them, he would still be riding by himself once they were out of sight.

And then he remembered what Mom said, and he rolled over to look out the window by his bed, up into the clear-as-glass New Mexico night.

"God?" he whispered. "I want to fight this battle for You. I think Olive needs help—and she's about the only kid of Yours I *can* help. Please—will you show me a way?"

He closed his eyes and waited to feel better. He didn't. All the anger he'd been stowing away churned up from his insides, and he was suddenly burying his face in his pillow and crying in hard, angry sobs that hurt as they jerked his chest and shouldered their way out of his throat. He cried until the sobs turned into big, shaky breaths and his mind sighed into an exhausted sleep.

Somewhere in its fog, he felt a presence beside him. He couldn't open his eyes, but he could feel a big hand on his back.

"Will sad," said a thick voice. "Not be sad, Will."

But there continued to be cause for sadness.

April 1 was Easter Day—and on that day there was word that the Allied invasion of Okinawa had begun. Everyone hoped it would bring them closer to the end of the war, but everyone also knew it would mean more men wounded or killed. The Armour's Star ham Mom splurged 39 cents a pound on for Easter dinner went largely uneaten that day—except by Abe.

More meals went to waste on April 6 and 7, when 355 kamikazes filled the air over the Pacific, sinking four American ships and damaging 25 more.

Almost two weeks later, on April 12, news came when the Hutchinsons were eating supper and listening to the radio that President Roosevelt had died late that afternoon. A "massive cerebral hemorrhage," the announcer said.

Mom shook her head as she set down her fork. "The poor man worked himself to death," she said.

Still another supper went uneaten.

The day of the funeral, it seemed that the whole nation came close to shutting down completely. There was silence over the airwaves and telephone lines during the service, in honor of the man who, along with England's Winston Churchill, was the "spokesman for freedom."

There was no school that day, and Mr. T. invited the children to spend the whole day at the ranch. Will heard him whisper to Mom, "They've seen enough sadness. Let them be kids."

Abe, too, had the day off. He still had trouble getting within six feet of a horse, so Miguel, Fawn, and Will hung out with him, playing hide and seek—not an easy game for big Abe, who had some difficulty concealing himself—and Red Rover—at which he excelled.

All morning, Will felt himself looking longingly out into the desert where he could be riding right now, looking for Olive, if it weren't for that rule box. Aside from wanting to know if she was all right, he couldn't help wondering if she knew everything that was happening in the world right now.

I think everybody has the right to know that we're winning the war, he thought, prickles popping up on the back of his neck. *And that the President has died!*

Even Olive knew that President Roosevelt had brought the nation out of the Depression. She had asked him if it was over, and he'd told her all about how amazing a President he had been. She would want to know that he had passed away.

The group finished up its third game of Red Rover, and they all sat down on hay bales outside the barn to try to think of something else to do.

"I sure wish we could go riding," Fawn mumbled, casting a sour glance at Abe.

Will nudged her with his elbow and frowned.

"I know, I know," she said.

They fell into a sullen silence, and Will went back to thinking. *If it just weren't for that stupid rule. No riding alone. I don't get it. I ride my bike alone all the time. I definitely walk alone. If I miss the bus, too bad—I walk to school—*

Suddenly it was as if everything stopped, including his heart. The only thing still running was one thought: *I can't ride alone, but nobody said I couldn't walk.*

Will could feel himself going cold, in spite of the April sun that was splashing its warmth against the adobe wall. Of course. Why hadn't he thought of it before? The only trick was to do it without any of them knowing. He closed his eyes and tried to formulate a plan before the opportunity slipped away.

"You are tired, Weel?" Miguel said.

That was it. Will feigned a yawn and stretched. "Yeah, I'm pretty tired. I think I'll climb up in the loft and take a nap."

"How can you be tired?" Fawn said. "It's not even noon yet!"

"I don't know," Will said. "I just am."

He stood up, stretched again, and headed inside the barn. He could feel a big presence behind him.

"No, Abe," he said. "You don't have to take a nap. You can stay up and play."

"Play games!" Abe said. He clapped his hands and turned to Miguel and Fawn, who both blinked at him.

"What would you like to play, my friend?" Miguel said.

"Games!" Abe said.

"Okay, I got one," Fawn said. "Abe, you be the horse and Miguel and I will ride you."

Abe immediately began to shake his head. "Horse. No. Abey no horse."

"No, silly," Fawn said. "You don't have to *ride* a horse—you get to *be* a horse."

Abe still didn't seem to be buying it. Fawn was getting down on her hands and knees to demonstrate as Will bade them all "good night" and tried not to appear too anxious as he hurried into the barn and up the ladder to the hayloft.

Sleep was the furthest thing from his mind, but he lay down on a pile of hay near the small window and pretended to be deep into a nap. Below, he could hear Fawn's shrieks and Miguel's quiet laughter and Abe's cries of "Abey! Horsie!"

It made him feel suddenly lonely. Why couldn't he just tell them about Olive and they could all go looking for her?

She told me not to, he thought. *She said that if I told anyone, she would hide so I'd never find her.*

Will grunted to himself. That kind of thing had never stopped him from doing exactly what he wanted to before. He sat up, hay draped around his shoulders. He was ready to go down and tell his friends everything and proclaim that they should saddle up—

But he sank back down into the hay, his heart like lead. Olive's father—Will had never heard a meaner-sounding man. That was the real reason he couldn't tell anyone.

So Will lay there for a while, pretending to sleep, while he listened to the sounds of his friends growing more carefree—and farther away. Finally, Will sat up and peeked out the window opening. Fawn, Abe, and Miguel were on the other side of the corral, Abe on all fours with the other two on his back. He was currently playing bucking bronco, amid happy squeals from his riders.

With a pang of sadness, Will stood up, brushed off the hay, and crept down the ladder and out the back door of the barn.

✛ ✛ ✛

Chapter Fourteen

*A*s Will took off across the desert at a dead run toward the spot where he had last seen Olive, he told himself he would be back before Miguel, Fawn, and Abe even knew he was missing.

I just hope they don't decide to come wake me up for lunch, he thought. He glanced anxiously up at the sky. The sun was only halfway to its high. He had at least a couple of hours. He just hoped the riding-on-Abe's-back game didn't wear out too quickly.

By the time Will climbed the hill where he'd parted from Olive, the sun was much closer to its noon position, and Will was breathing hard. What seemed like nothing on a horse was a workout on foot.

But as Will reached the top of the hill, his energy came back in a rush. He was here; he was close. Maybe in a few minutes, it would all turn out to be worth it.

Once he settled himself on the crest, though, he wasn't quite sure what to do next. In the past, Olive had always been the one to find *him.*

That's because she was always spying on me, Will thought. *But I bet she's stopped looking for me. I bet she thinks I've forgotten about her.*

After all, ever since he'd been focusing more on Abe, the kids hadn't ridden up this far.

Or maybe her father found out she was watching for me. Maybe he—

Will stood up abruptly, sending pebbles skittering down the side of the hill and bouncing off the rocks. He couldn't think that way. He had to go farther and look harder. He had to be sure.

He and Miguel and Fawn had never been farther than this spot. But Olive's house or whatever it was she lived in wasn't within view, so it was obvious he was going to have to go over the next hill. The sun was getting close to announcing noon pretty soon, but he gave up on trying to get back before lunch. He was out here now; there was no turning back.

Smearing the dust from his forehead with his sleeve, Will started his trek down the back side of the hill. From a cliff above and to the right, a crow squawked at him, probably complaining that Will was disturbing the red dust, which puffed out from the sides of his boots as he walked. Ahead, a chipmunk sat upright on a rock, cocked his head at Will, and scampered away.

Spring was well established now, and wild flowers waved their wands in the wind on all sides of him.

I wish I did have some kind of magic wand, Will thought.

And then he shook his head. *Sorry, God. I don't need magic. I have You. Mom says if somebody's hurting somebody, we have to step in. It's like a rule, right from the box. Your box.*

Shaking off the nagging thought that somehow God's rule seemed to butt heads with Mr. T.'s rule, Will reminded himself that nobody had said anything about *walking* alone and kept on.

The next hill was steeper and more thickly coated with gravel, which made it trickier to climb. Will did most of it on hands and knees, so that he was caked with red dust by the time he reached the top. But one look beyond him from that vantage point and everything was forgotten, including the gravel stings on his palms.

There, just at the bottom of the hill in the midst of a stand of cottonwoods, was a house. It actually looked like two large metal toolsheds stuck together and bonded by one rusty-red metal roof. Will might not have known it was a house at all if he hadn't seen Olive sitting cross-legged on a sagging, makeshift front porch, reading a book.

It was all Will could do not to call out to her, but the memory of her father's voice, carrying from this place over two hills as if he had been two feet away, stopped him.

Instead, Will picked up a handful of gravel and hurled it at the flimsy sheet of metal that formed a roof over the porch. As the stones hit like a spattering of applause, Olive looked up—right at Will.

She untangled herself and stood up. She put her hands on her hips as she stared at him, then shook her head and disappeared into the house, leaving only the blank, gaping hole of the doorway.

No—don't go! Will wanted to shout after her.

He ventured a few steps down the hill, his eyes on the fence that surrounded the front of the house and disappeared into the trees behind it. For a ramshackle house, it certainly had a sturdy fence, built of thick wood posts and covered with wire mesh. It was as high as the house if not higher, and every few yards all the way around hung an old tire with the words KEEP OUT! painted on it in white letters. When Will got about halfway down the hill, he stopped and looked at the whole setup in despair.

It'd take me some time to climb that, he thought, his heart sagging. *Long enough for that monster to see me.*

By now, Olive's father had taken on gigantic proportions in his mind. Will could almost picture him, his mean mouth like a gash in his face, his eyes red and fiery, his hands forever doubled into fists. He decided right then that if he did get to Olive, he was going to take her back to the ranch, even if he had to tie her up.

But it was obvious he was never going to get to her. As he sat on the side of the hill, careful to keep himself concealed behind an especially fluffy juniper, Will never took his eyes off of the house, but Olive didn't reappear in the doorway. The place was silent as a tomb.

That image made him shudder, and Will was searching his head for another one when a sudden rush of gravel slid down beside him. Will tried to sort out his legs and get himself to his feet, but before he could accomplish that, there was someone sitting beside him.

It was Olive.

"It's you!" Will said. He knew he sounded idiotic, but it was what came out.

"You were expecting maybe Geronimo?" she said.

"Who?" Will said.

Two dimples appeared on Olive's square chin. "I can see you haven't gotten any smarter since I last saw you."

"How did you get up here?" Will glanced behind him at the top of the hill. "You were down there and then—you were up here."

"Catching you from behind, I might add." She shook her mane of dark hair. "I'd explain, simple head, but it would take too long for you to get it. And besides, we'd better get out of sight."

Will ignored her insults and followed her around the side of the hill where a formation of rocks formed a perfect hiding place. Will climbed in after Olive and settled himself in, out of the sun and the wind and the possible peering eyes of Olive's father.

Still, he had to ask, "Is he gonna come looking for you?"

"Not for a while," Olive said. "I checked before I climbed out the back window. He's out in the field." She nudged Will with the very scuffed toe of her boot. "Where have you been?"

Will explained to her about the new rule and about Abe. She drank it in as she always had, as if she were starved for news. When Will filled her in about Iwo Jima and Okinawa and Roosevelt and the kamikazes, her eyes widened to twice their size. For a few minutes, Will felt a little bit powerful. It gave him the nerve, finally, to say, "Look, Olive, you gotta tell me what's going on with you and your father. I was thinking you were dead up here or something!"

Olive made a face, but it wasn't very convincing. Will could see the fear she was trying to keep from flickering through her eyes.

"How can I be sure you won't tell anyone?" she said.

"Because I *walked* all the way up here to make sure you were all right. By myself."

Still, Olive surveyed him for a full minute before she sighed and said, "Oh, all right."

"Then give," Will said.

Olive sat with her knees propped up, leaning her forearms and her chin on them. She didn't look at Will as she began.

"When the war first started—you know, when Pearl Harbor was attacked—"

"Yeah."

"My father wasn't like most other people. He thought it was wrong for America to get into the war. He said it was just an excuse to get us out of the Depression—you know, a way to give a bunch of people jobs."

"Is he one of those religious people who doesn't believe in war?" Will said. "What do you call them?"

"Conscientious objectors," Olive said. "Kind of, I guess, only he isn't religious. He doesn't even believe in God anymore."

"Yikes," Will said.

"So anyway, he was a teacher at St. Michael's High School which didn't pay all that much, so when the war started, my mother was able to get a job at a factory to help with the war effort."

"I bet he didn't like that."

"Are you kidding? Every morning they would have a fight about her going to work. She was so proud that her factory had one of those Army-Navy E pennants flying over it, because that showed that they had a good record for supporting the war. He would threaten to go over there and tear it down."

"Did he?"

Olive shook her head. "She only worked there for four months before she had an accident with one of the machines."

Her voice trailed off. Will waited, twisting and untwisting his fingers until his hands were clammy.

"After she died," Olive finally went on, "my father went a little crazy. He would stand by the newspapers in the LaFonda Hotel, and every time somebody came by to buy one, he would tell them the paper was full of lies about the war."

"I bet that was embarrassing."

"Not as embarrassing as when they fired him from his job at St. Michael's for telling the students that President Roosevelt was rubbing his hands together every time an American boy was killed overseas because that meant more money."

"That's doesn't make any sense!" Will said.

"Oh, he stopped making sense a long time ago," Olive said. "That's why they ran him out of town three years ago this month. He brought me up here and we've been here ever since.

He says the world—and especially the war—can't hurt us up here."

"So that's why you'd get in trouble if he knew you were even talking to me."

"You could say that." Her voice was as dry as the desert itself. "He's just afraid somebody from Santa Fe's going to find out we're living up here and make trouble like they did before." She shrugged. "When he gets afraid, he yells."

"Did he find out about me, that day you came home hurt?"

Olive shook her head. "Not exactly. I told him I fell into a mine shaft—but I'm not sure he believed me. He'd never hit me or anything—I don't want you thinking that—but he hasn't let me outside the fence since then. I can't stand seeing that stupid thing, penning me in, so I've mostly stayed inside the house." She grinned at him. "I've been bored out of my skull. I kept wishing you'd show up so we could argue about something. Funny thing how I decided to sit on the porch today. I must've known you were coming."

"Do you believe in God?" Will asked.

Olive gave him a bewildered look. "Where did that come from?" she said.

"I just wondered. My mom would say the reason you came out on the porch was because of God."

"I haven't noticed Him coming around here too much," Olive said, in that same dry voice. "I wish He would. I'm about to go crazy myself."

"So you do believe in Him?" Will said.

Olive didn't answer. Instead, she snapped her head up, eyes on the top of the hill. Will looked up too, in time to see Fawn, Abe, and Miguel looking down at them.

Olive was immediately on Will, her eyes narrowed. "You said you wouldn't tell!"

She started to get up, but Will grabbed her wrist. "I didn't tell—honest. They musta followed me here."

"We did," Fawn said, strolling easily down the side of the hill with Abe staggering behind her. "You'd make a lousy Indian, Will. You left a path so plain, it was like footprints in the snow."

Will looked at Miguel, who was sheepishly trailing Abe and obviously trying to avoid Will's eyes. When he did catch them, Miguel said, "I tried to persuade her not to follow you, my friend, but she was afraid for you."

"I wasn't afraid," Fawn said. "I just figured you'd done something clumsy and you'd need us to rescue you."

"So he's always been clumsy, huh?"

Will looked at Olive in amazement. She was looking at Fawn, still with guarded eyes, but with the hint of a grin around her lips.

"Yeah, I'm always having to get him out of some kind of trouble," Fawn said.

Olive watched Fawn for a minute before she answered. Fawn, of course, stood there, open-faced, ready to either be her friend or take her on.

"I guess there's a Keep-Will-Out-of-Trouble Club," Olive said finally. She shrugged. "I guess I became a member when I found him in a—"

"Never mind!" Will said.

Olive looked at him. Slowly she smiled. The fear was fading from her eyes. "Really, Smart Will," she said, "remember your manners."

Fawn snickered. Will glared at her.

It suddenly seemed as if Olive had made a decision. She sat back on her elbows as if she were in an armchair and said, "Aren't you going to introduce me to your friends?"

Will was having a little trouble keeping up, but he turned to Miguel and said, "This is my friend Miguel Otero."

"Pleased to meet you," Miguel said and put out his hand for

Olive to shake. She looked amused, but she didn't laugh. Will was grateful to her for that.

"And this is Abe." He lowered his voice. "He's big but he's not—"

"I understand." Olive put both of her hands around one of Abe's and looked up at him. "Hi," she said. "You want to be friends?"

Abe gave one of his gleeful gurgles, the kind that let spit escape from the corners of his mouth. It didn't seem to faze Olive at all. Abe squeezed himself into the rock place and settled in beside her. Will knew it was going to take heaven and earth to move him out of there.

"And this is Fawn," Will said.

"I'm sort of his sister," Fawn said. "Not by blood, but his mom is my mom until my own mom gets out of the hospital and my dad gets back from the war. Then . . ." Fawn paused and fingered one of her braids. "Then I guess she'll always be my mom anyway, you know, sort of."

Olive hadn't taken her eyes off of Fawn since she'd started to talk. Will thought they looked shinier than usual, in a liquid kind of way.

"You're so lucky," Olive said to Fawn. "I hope you appreciate how lucky you are."

Fawn, however, wasn't in an appreciating mood. She turned on Will, her eyes flashing. "So how come you kept her to yourself?" she said. "She's the girl you almost ran over with Cisco that one day, huh?"

"Yeah, but—"

"Yeah, but what?" Fawn said, planting her hands savagely on her hips. "You just wanted to keep her all for yourself! I know how you are. You never—"

"Wait," Olive said. "It's not his fault. I wouldn't let him tell anybody or I'd get in trouble."

Fawn was immediately fascinated.

That's the thing about Fawn, Will thought as Olive repeated the story about her father. *She changes moods faster than I can change my clothes.*

Will watched with his chin dropped to his chest as Olive told Fawn and the boys the rest of her story. It was as if once she decided she could trust them, she couldn't hold back anymore.

By the time she had finished the tale, Fawn was hooked. Between her and Abe, Will wasn't sure they'd get back to the ranch before sundown. In fact, as they all continued to talk—and eat the tortillas and corn bread and salted peanuts from a small bag which Abe, naturally, had stuffed in his pockets—Will began to grow uneasy about how long they'd been away from the ranch.

"We oughta think about getting back," he said at one point. "Mr. T. and Mom and everybody's gonna be worried about us."

"No," Miguel said. "We told them we were playing hide and seek." His dark eyes grew innocent. "It was not a lie."

"I love the way you talk," Olive said to him. "I love the way all of you talk. Do you think you could come back and see me— I mean, every day—or so?"

There was no hesitation. Everyone agreed heartily, and no one more than Abe.

"Uh, pal," Will said to him. "That means you're going to have to learn how to ride a horse."

His big face clouded so quickly that Will wished he hadn't said anything, but Olive was already shaking her head.

"If he's afraid of the horses," she said, "you could come and get me and we could all ride to a secret place I know that Abe could walk to."

"Wouldn't your dad get suspicious, though?" Will said. "If you left every day at the same time? I thought you had to stay inside the fence."

"That was only temporary. And my father has something new to occupy him right now," Olive said. "Besides, I think I've convinced him there's nobody around."

It was Miguel's turn to look stormy. "You must lie to your father?"

Olive lifted her chin, as if she were defying her father right that very moment, to his face. "I don't think it counts when your father isn't in his right mind," she said. "And if I don't have some contact with the outside world, I won't be in mine much longer."

Once again Will saw that shine in her eyes, and he knew what it was. She was about to cry.

The kids left her very reluctantly that afternoon, and they were only able to tear Abe away by promising that he would see Olive again, many times. She followed them for a while and showed them the secret spot near the ranch where Abe could meet them all—a cave carved by time and perhaps some ancient Indians, right in the side of a rocky cliff. Will noticed that it wasn't far from the mine shaft he had fallen into, but Olive didn't say a word. It was odd to him: the longer she spent with Will, Miguel, Fawn, and Abe, the less sharp her answers were and the less she teased him.

He didn't miss it at all.

Olive's eyes were the shiniest ever when she left them at the last bend before the ranch, and Will was sure she would cry as she ran back home.

He was close to tears himself that night as he lay in bed, the radio chattering in the kitchen below about Okinawa. He felt like fighting again, but not over things like riding alone that suddenly didn't seem to matter so much.

All this death caused by fighting, he thought, as the radio announcer droned on. *I want to fight a fight that's not about death.*

"God," he whispered. "I want to fight so Olive can really live."

✝ ✦ ✝

Chapter Fifteen

*T*hey met Olive every day after that. Will figured her father must *really* be occupied with whatever his new interest was, because she never missed a day with them. Each day, the kids scooped her up from the second hill away from her house and rode with her to the secret cave, where not long after that, Abe would find them, grinning gleefully, always with his pockets stuffed with snacks.

They had the best times together that Will could remember having in a long while with anyone.

Fawn brought the bubble gum she'd been storing up and they had a bubble-blowing contest.

Some days they played baseball with sticks and the ball Will brought in his saddlebag. Other days it was a tic-tac-toe tournament, done in the dirt.

Will was good at telling the plots of Alfred Hitchcock thrillers, which Olive loved, but which scared Abe too much, so he only did that before Abe arrived. Then they would switch to contests to see who could stuff the most Tootsie Rolls in his or her mouth and still be able to say "chubby bunny," or who could actually crack the rock on the side of the cliff with stone hammers they made themselves, under Olive's teaching.

"I think you must know everything," Fawn said to her one day as they were hammering away.

"Huh," Olive said. "There's not much else to do out here *but* learn. I'd go nuts if I didn't have books."

Will stopped slamming at the cliff and set his hammer down as he looked out over the vast expanse of hills, all polka-dotted with junipers and piñons.

"It must be nice sometimes, though," he said. "It's so quiet. You don't have anybody saying, 'Go to school, make good grades, follow all the rules inside the box.' "

"Maybe it would be nice," Olive said, "if there wasn't another whole world I was missing out on, or if I had somebody I could share it with." She leaned against the cliff wall and toyed with her stone hammer. "It got better when you came up here, Will, and now that I have all of you, it's the best it's ever been. I think I might make it now."

Suddenly there was a loud crack, and they all jumped, including Abe, who was staring at a long gash he had just cut into the rock.

"You did it, Abe!" Will said.

Abe grinned, earlobe to earlobe, and Olive squeezed his arm warmly. He dropped his hammer as he gurgled down at her.

"*Cielo bueno!*" Miguel cried suddenly. "Look what he has found!"

Miguel was staring into the crack Abe had made, his eyes like dinner plates.

"What?" Fawn said. "Is it gold?"

Will rolled his eyes.

"No," Miguel said. "I think it is better." He looked at Will. "Better for us, my friend."

Will hurried over and peered into the crack. Miguel pointed with a shaking finger at a small strip of plain brown stone which was different from the surrounding rock. It had a tiny vein of blue-green winding through it.

"It's turquoise!" Will said.

Olive joined him. "It couldn't possibly be," she said. "The Spaniards took all the turquoise out of this area years ago—" She stopped and grinned up at Will. "But it looks like they missed this little spot."

Miguel sat down and quickly fashioned another tool out of a piece of sharp rock, again with Olive's help and with Fawn's inquisitive nose poked right into the whole process. Miguel and Will took turns digging around the strip of stone until they had a piece out just big enough to cover the end of Will's thumb. The turquoise in it looked waxy and was soft to the touch, but it was real, Olive assured them of that.

"Let's dig for more!" Fawn said.

"You're kidding, right?" Will said. "All I heard for weeks out of you was whining because you were sick of digging."

"That was different," she said, setting her chin.

She was right, Will thought. Everything was different with Olive around.

He was deciding whether to actually say that out loud, when Olive suddenly put her finger to her lips and got very still. Everyone did the same, including Abe, who stuffed his fist into his mouth for good measure.

At first, Will wasn't sure what it was they were listening for—and then he heard it. Bushes below the cave were rustling, as if someone were moving toward them. In the absolute silence, he could hear that someone breathing.

Olive's face went white, and she seemed to be frozen to her spot. Will put a hand up to tell the rest of them to stay put, and then he crept slowly toward the opening of the cave and peered out. He couldn't hold back the laugh that burst out of him.

"Who is it?" Fawn hissed.

"It's a steer!" Will said.

"A steer?" Fawn joined him at the opening and looked back over her shoulder at the others. "It *is!*" she said, as if Will's report required confirmation.

"It must have wandered away from the ranch," Will said. "But that's strange. Mr. T. has the ranch hands watching those cattle like hawks."

By now, Olive had crowded her way into the cave opening to see, and she shook her mane of hair. "That's one of my father's steers," she said.

Will stared at her. "Your father has cattle?"

"He just got them. That's why I can get away so much. He's all wrapped up in being a cowboy now." She rolled her dark eyes.

"Why is your steer so far away from its field?" Miguel said.

"He's new," Olive said. "The poor thing probably doesn't know how to get home yet. I'd better take care of this."

She crawled out of the cave and climbed deftly down the cliff, like the mountain girl she had become. But the minute she moved toward the steer, the animal wailed and trotted into the trees.

"Come on, boy," she said. "You have to go home." She bent at the waist and held out her hand. "See? I have a Tootsie Roll for you."

Will snickered to himself. He had finally found something Olive couldn't do.

"We know how to get him home," Will said. "We've seen them do it at the ranch enough times."

"I'll get behind and give him a slap on the rump," Fawn said.

"Then once we get him out of the trees we can herd him home with the horses."

Olive looked at him, her eyes doubtful. "Have you ever done it before?"

"We're a little closer to having done it than you are," Will said. He looked at Fawn. "You and Miguel are better riders than me, though. I'll get him going and you two do the herding."

"But you can't come all the way to the house," Olive said. "Just get him to the first hill and I'll get my father to take him the rest of the way."

Abe let out a whimper, and Olive took the time to go over to him and assure him that she would see them all again tomorrow.

"You won't see me," Fawn said. "Margretta Dietrich's coming through Lamy tomorrow on her way up to Chicago for some meeting, and Mama Hutchie says I have to go with her to the train station so she can talk to me about my mother. See, my mother's in a hospital, and Margretta, she's been making sure she's all right—"

"Pray?" Abe said suddenly.

Olive smiled at him. "Of course we'll pray tomorrow," she said. "As long as you bring me more Tootsie Rolls."

Abe nodded until Will was sure his head would roll off. He was still nodding as Will made his way through the trees, talking softly to the steer the way he'd heard the ranch hands do it.

He'd also seen them give the cattle's rear ends a wide berth, so he put a few feet between himself and this animal's kicking range, murmuring to him all the while. But the murmuring stopped when he caught sight of his right flank.

There, branded into his flesh, were the letters TR. *Tarantino Ranch.*

"We are ready, my friend," he heard Miguel say.

Woodenly, Will gave the steer a slap on the brand, and he moved noisily out of the trees. Miguel made some kind of noise out of the side of his mouth, and with much loud complaining, the steer allowed himself to be herded down the hill into the meadow below. Olive was sitting behind Fawn on Virgy, holding on and laughing into the wind as they rode.

But Will wasn't laughing.

Why does Olive's father have a steer with Mr. T.'s brand on it? he wondered.

"Sad, Will?" Abe said anxiously.

"No, I'm not sad, pal," Will said. "Let's you and me walk back to the ranch. I'll just lead Cisco—nobody's going to ride."

Abe nodded, but he kept well away from Cisco as they made their way back to the ranch. Abe was keeping such a watchful eye on the horse, he didn't bother about conversation, which gave Will time to think it over and sort it through.

Maybe she just thought *that was one of her dad's steers,* he thought. *She said he just got them. Maybe she just doesn't know one from another.*

Or did her father steal it from Mr. T. and she didn't even know it?

Or did *she know it?*

Will shook his head. That last one wasn't even an option. Olive couldn't possibly know her father was a cattle thief and then hang around with people who were friends with the very person he stole them from.

But the thoughts wouldn't leave him alone. Apparently, they wouldn't leave Miguel alone, either. That night up in Will's room, as they were putting the final touches on their turquoise mine model, including the piece of actual turquoise they'd found that day, Miguel was unusually quiet. Finally, when the last piece was glued on, he looked at Will with sad eyes and said, "Did you see the brand on that steer?"

Will was at first startled, but he nodded. "Yeah," he said. "I did."

"What are you thinking?" Miguel said. "Are you thinking her father—"

"Yeah, only she doesn't know it. I know she doesn't!" Will said.

Miguel studied the model, but Will knew his mind was far away. "Perhaps she made a mistake," he said. "Perhaps she only thought that was her father's steer."

"That's what I thought!" Will said. He hoped that was true. He wanted it to be true.

"I think we must find out," Miguel said.

"You mean, go find the rest of his herd?"

Will nodded.

"We're gonna have to do it without Olive, though. I don't want her to think we even suspect her father." He looked at Miguel. "You think Fawn can keep her mouth shut?"

"We will not have Fawn with us tomorrow," Miguel said. "She is going to the train station with your mother, remember?"

Will could feel a grin spreading over his face. "Yeah," he said. "I remember. I think this has to be one of those things God sets up, you know?"

All day long the next day, Will assured himself—and Miguel—that they were going to find one Tarantino steer in the midst of others that had never seen the inside of Mr. T.'s fences. But as they left the ranch on the backs of Cisco and Hilachas, Will's hands were sweaty on the reins. Even Cisco was skittish, balking at every lizard and tossing his head at random, as if he could feel Will's anxiety.

"Easy, boy," Will said to him, as much to soothe himself as the horse. After all, they were going to spy on property that belonged to a man whom even his own daughter was afraid of.

The first problem was in finding where he might be keeping his herd. When Olive had talked about him being "out in the field" she had pointed in a direction vaguely north of the tin shack they lived in. Will and Miguel decided it must be below the mesa that stood behind the shack. Practically holding their breaths, they let the horses pick their way up the back side of the small mesa and carry them to the top where they could look down into the field below. The only problem was that the flat top of the mesa was almost bare, which meant they could be seen for miles. Miguel suggested they leave the horses tied to the few trees that did exist and go the rest of the way on foot.

"We can lie flat on the ground to look down," Miguel said. "Then we will not be so conspic—conspic—what is the word?"

"We won't stick out like a sore thumb," Will said.

Miguel flashed a smile. "That is the word, my friend."

Once the horses were safely tied, Miguel and Will crawled across the mesa, which was no more than a hundred yards wide, and flattened themselves on their stomachs to look down into the field below.

Sure enough, there, grazing on a sickly pasture, were three cattle, all exactly like the one they had discovered the day before. From their lofty observation point, Will couldn't clearly see the brands on their rears as they grazed on chamisa and sage and switched their tails and stamped at the flies. But they did have brands—and they had the same shape as Mr. T.'s.

"I gotta believe those are Mr. T.'s cattle," Will said. "But where do you think the rest of them are?"

Miguel gave him a quizzical look.

"Mr. T.'s had over 50 head stolen," Will said. "Unless Olive and her dad have eaten all that beef already, they gotta be somewhere."

"And who was with him when he took them?" Miguel said. "You told Señor T. there were two men stealing the cattle."

"Two men in masks," Will said. He felt a sudden chill, and he didn't say to Miguel what slithered through his mind like an evil snake: *Was one of those bandits a girl in a mask?*

"Come on," he said quickly to chase the thought out. "We better go meet Olive or she'll think we're not coming today."

But before Will could even begin to get up, there was a click behind them, and a voice said, "Turn around slowly and you won't get hurt."

✞ ✦ ✞

Chapter Sixteen

*W*ill started to whip around but something hard pressed against his back.

"I said turn slowly!" the voice said.

There was an edge to it that Will would have recognized anywhere. It was the same voice that had shouted at Olive over two hills. It was her father.

Will and Miguel both turned slowly to face a square-shouldered, Spanish-looking man with a thin moustache and small, darting eyes. The eyes scared Will even more than the voice. They looked intelligent, the way Mr. T.'s did, but they had a wildness in them that made Will fear for what the man might do next. It seemed it could be anything from giving them a lecture on the evils of trespassing to hurling both boys off the side of the mesa. It might be a good idea, Will thought, to try to explain—something.

"Please, sir," Will said. "We weren't doing anything wrong. We were just—"

"Quiet!" the man said. "I will ask the questions, and I want the answer to those questions and nothing more. Am I understood?"

Will nodded. He could feel Miguel shaking beside him.

"Are those your horses?" the man said, jerking his head toward the trees where Cisco and Hilachas were munching on leaves as if their riders *weren't* being interrogated by a madman.

"They belong to my mother," Miguel said.

"Where is your mother?" He gestured toward Will with the gun. "And yours?"

"My mother works. She's a teacher," Will said.

He didn't wait for Miguel to explain about his parent, which Will thought was a good thing. Although his mind was spinning, he did know one thing: If Olive's father found out they were connected in any way to the ranch, he might just push them over the side after all.

"What business do you have here?" the man said.

"Um . . . no business," Will said. "We were just hanging around. We're kids—that's what we do."

"Don't be a smart aleck with me, boy," the man said. "I don't take impertinence off of children."

Will wasn't sure what impertinence was, but he *was* sure that he disliked this man more than ever. The thought of Olive having to spend every minute with him—him and no one else—was boiling his blood. The urge to fight rammed its way right into his head.

"I wasn't being a smart aleck!" Will said. "This isn't private property. We got as much right to be here as anybody!"

The man readjusted the gun in his hands and put his face close to Will's. From behind him, Miguel pushed Will out of the way so that the gun was now pointed directly into his nose. Will could see the hair that hung below Miguel's hat shivering with the fear he must be feeling, but Miguel said, "Sir, we are at work on a project for our school. Do you know where we might find any turquoise?"

The man looked Miguel over carefully before he spat out a laugh. "Turquoise?" he said. "You're about a century too late for finding turquoise!"

This time he spat out real spit, on the ground off to the side, and then he lowered the gun.

"Get your horses and leave the premises, both of you. There's no turquoise here."

Will opened his mouth to argue, but Miguel grabbed his arm and pulled him, not letting go until they'd reached the horses. Olive's father was still watching them as they left the mesa behind.

"You shoulda let me give him a piece of my mind, Miguel!" Will said when they were well out of range.

"I was afraid I would soon be picking a piece of your mind up off of the ground, my friend," Miguel said.

Will shrugged and rode on. Miguel was right, of course, but that didn't calm his anger—*or* solve his problem.

Mr. T. should be told where some of his stolen cattle were. But if Will told him, Olive's father, and maybe even Olive herself, would be in trouble.

I don't care if he rots in jail, he thought. *But then what happens to Olive?*

If he could just talk to Olive about it and find out if she knew the cattle her father had were stolen. That would help him decide what to do.

But how was he going to see her now? Her father was sure to have her locked up already, knowing there were kids from the "outside world" roaming around. And even if she did get out and Will met her, what if her father caught him again? He was sure he wouldn't let him off so easily a second time.

"I did not like that man's eyes," Miguel said.

"That 'man' was Olive's father; I'm sure of it," Will said. "And I didn't like them either—they were strange, like he was crazy or something."

"There was a crazy man in Chimayo once," Miguel said. "He had the same eyes—"

Miguel went on to describe them, but Will's attention was caught on the thought he'd just had. One of the bandits, the one who had knocked Will down, had been cross-eyed. Olive's father's eyes were indeed haunting, but they weren't crossed, and neither were Olive's. It was for sure Olive wasn't one of the bandits—and perhaps neither was her father.

Will tried to talk himself into that. It would make everything so much easier. But he was hard to convince. He knew he had to talk to Olive.

But how's it going to happen today? he thought when they were back at the stables and Will was brushing Cisco's fly-bitten coat. *I have to get home and be there when Abe gets in from school since Mom's not going to be there.*

And who knew how long she and Fawn would be in Lamy? It was 20 miles from Santa Fe, which could keep them out past dark.

It seemed hopeless, and yet as he and Miguel rode their bikes back to town and parted ways at Canyon Road, a plan was already forming in his mind.

God, I sure hope this is You, he prayed. *I have to help Olive out of this mess she doesn't even know she's in. I gotta fight for her.*

He pedaled madly up the driveway and tossed his bike against the back porch. Abe met him at the back door, a huge grin on his face and the crumbs of more than one cookie on his lips. No wonder Mom always liked to be there when he got home. Otherwise, there would probably be no groceries left.

Will was surprised to see him so early. Usually it was dark before Abe got home.

"Did they kick you out of school, pal?" Will said with a grin.

Abe's face was stormy. "No kick!"

"I was kidding—jeepers. How come you're home so early?"

"Flood," Abe said.

"What are you talking about? It isn't even raining."

Abe shook his head hard. "School—flood."

"Oh," Will said. "The plumbing again, huh?" The Opportunity School ran on so little money, it was amazing it had plumbing at all. Will pushed that aside, however. He had a golden opportunity, right in front of him.

"Hey, Abe!" he said. "You wanna go back out to the ranch with me? I'll tow you on my bike."

Abe clapped his hands and said, "Play games!"

"Yeah," Will said. "Play games."

I wish we were *playing games,* he thought as he struggled out of the driveway with Abe hanging over on the back of the bike. It might have made more sense for Abe to pedal and Will to ride on the fender, but Will didn't want to take any chances with Abe at the handlebars. He didn't want to arrive with Abe all shaken up—and then have to tell him he was going to ride with Will on a horse.

This is going to work, he told himself as they neared the ranch with Abe squealing happily behind him. *Abe won't know what Olive and I are talking about, and I won't be alone out there. I won't be breaking out of the box.*

He *would* have to tell Mr. T. they were going, which might be risky, since it wasn't far from sunset. But to do it without telling him was even riskier. That could mean the end of horseback riding altogether.

Olive might be worth it. He was sure she was. But so were Mr. T. and his mom and Señora Otero, who would all go insane if Will and Abe were discovered "missing." Besides, if something were to happen out there, it would be good for someone to know where they were.

But nothing's going to happen, he told himself firmly. *I'll talk to Olive and it'll be all straightened out and I'll be laughing at myself an hour from now.*

After all, there might just be some other reason why Mr. T.'s steer had ended up in Olive's father's pasture.

When they got to the ranch, Abe got off the bike and bounded into the house looking for Señora Otero while Will headed for the stable. A few minutes later, as Will was saddling Cisco, Abe reappeared with a long face.

"What's wrong, pal?" Will said.

Abe shook his head.

"What do you mean, no? Wasn't Señora Otero there?"

Abe shook his head again, and Will laughed. "That means no snacks for you, huh? Too bad. Go find Mr. T. for me, would you?"

But that errand, too, brought Abe up empty. It seemed there was nobody around but Gabby, and even he seemed to have his mind on something else when Will asked him where everybody was.

"They're all out lookin' for rustlers," Gabby said. "Mr. T. done lost 10 more head last night. He ain't got that many to lose . . ."

Gabby's voice went down to a mutter as he turned and went toward the tack room.

"Abe and I are going out for a short ride," Will said to his back.

"Uh-huh," Gabby said.

Will was going to repeat it, just to make sure Gabby had heard him, but he felt a tugging at his shirt and turned around to see Abe standing there, his fist crammed into his mouth and his eyes swimming with fear.

"What's wrong, pal?" Will said.

"Abey. Horse. No!"

He tried to stick the other fist into his mouth as well, but Will grabbed his wrist.

"No, Abe, it's okay," Will said. "You aren't going to ride by yourself. You're going to be on Cisco with me. All you have to do is hang on, just like on the bike!"

But Abe continued to shake his head, no small feat with two hands stuck in his mouth.

"Come on, pal, just this once," Will said. "I have to talk to Olive. I won't ride fast, I promise. No fooling around—"

He stopped. Abe had removed one fist and was working on the other. His eyes were dancing.

"Olive?" he said. "Olive and Abey?"

Will could feel himself grinning. "Yeah," he said. "Olive and Abey. And the sooner you get on that horse, the sooner you'll see her."

Although Abe would have let Will ride *him* out onto the desert—he was that excited at the prospect of seeing Olive—he still had to coax him onto Cisco. Even then, Abe clung to Will as if they were both about to be launched into outer space.

It was maddening to have to ride so slowly, but Will kept the horse at a stately pace. He glanced anxiously at the sky every other minute to try and calculate how much daylight they had left. Staying out with the horses after sunset was going to land him in big trouble, he was sure.

God, I'm not just fighting to be ornery this time, Will prayed as they rode with painstaking slowness. *I'm really trying to help Olive. I really have to get to her—fast.*

Fast did not at all describe their pace, but finally they reached the spot where he and Miguel and Fawn always picked Olive up. She was nowhere to be seen, and even when Will whispered her name, she didn't come. It didn't help that Abe was whimpering behind him and almost squeezing the air out of him. That was perhaps why he jumped when Olive stepped out from behind a large boulder and said, "You're a little late, aren't you?"

Abe leapt off the horse, tumbling to the ground with a thud and sending Cisco whinnying and stepping sideways. He threw his arms around Olive, who hugged him and stroked his hair as if he were five. For some reason he couldn't account for, Will got a lump in his throat. Maybe it was because Olive was so good, and what he was about to tell her was so bad.

"Hey, Abe," Will said as he dismounted and looped Cisco's reins loosely over a piñon pine branch. "Would you be our lookout?"

Abe nodded, but Will could tell by the look on his face that he had no idea what Will was talking about. Will led him to a spot about a hundred yards away, where the trees were somewhat thick and there were several rock formations jutting out of the ground.

"Kneel down right here," Will said, "just like you're praying. If anybody comes around, you just throw this that way." He handed Abe a fairly hefty stone and pointed to where Olive was standing. "We'll be talking over there," Will said. "We'll hear if you throw the stone. And don't move from here. Stay until I come get you. Got it?"

Abe nodded enthusiastically. Will still wasn't sure how much of that he'd gotten, but there wasn't time to repeat it the necessary 12 times. He patted Abe's arm and walked away.

"Abe and Olive?" Abe whispered. "Pray?"

"Yeah, pal," Will said. "Later."

But he was praying right now as he went back to Olive—praying that God liked the battle he had chosen and was going to help him fight it.

The minute he reached her, Olive pulled Will behind the boulder she'd emerged from. The light was fading, but even at that, Will could see that her face was dead white.

"Uh-oh," Will said.

"Yes, uh-oh!" Olive hissed. "My father came in madder than *ever* and told me he'd found two boys spying on our cow pasture from the mesa. I had to act like I didn't know who he was talking about, but I'm sure he didn't believe me." Will could see her swallowing hard. "I don't think we can take any more chances. I'm going to have to stop meeting with all of you—any of you. It's too dangerous."

Will could feel his eyes bulging. "No!" he said. He tried to keep his voice low, but it suddenly seemed to have a mind of its own. "He's never gonna find us again. We only went up there to check the cattle. We were exposed up on the mesa. That won't happen again!"

"Why in the world would you want to see my father's cattle? He has all of three, and they're getting skinnier by the day. By the time we ever eat them, there won't be any meat on them."

"That's just it," Will said. "They aren't his cattle. They belong to Mr. Tarantino—the man who owns the ranch where our horses are."

Olive shook her dark mane of hair. "No, they're my father's," she said. "I saw him give money for them. He bought them—" Her voice stopped abruptly, and her eyes narrowed at him. "What is that you're saying, Will?"

"I don't exactly know what I'm saying," Will said. "I just know we saw some rustlers stealing Mr. T.'s cattle, and—"

"And you think my father did it?"

"They were stolen, and he has them," Will said. "And I don't care if he did—I just want to make sure you know about it because if the police find out or something, you might have to go to an orphanage—"

Olive cut him off by standing straight up. The face that looked down at him was furious. "My father might be a little crazy," she said, "but he is *not* a thief! How dare you come around here accusing him?"

"I'm not accusing him—I'm trying to protect *you!*"

"Well, thank you very much, but I do not *need* your protection!"

Before Will could stop her, Olive turned on her heel with a swirl of wild black hair and disappeared into what was now gray dusk.

"Olive!" Will hissed after her. But there was no answer. She was gone.

He had the urge to run after her, but in what direction? And with darkness falling fast, he really had no choice but to collect Abe and head back for the ranch.

I did the best I could, God, he thought. *But it definitely wasn't good enough.*

He was still mulling over what he could have said differently that would have kept Olive from going off like that when he reached the spot where he had left Abe.

"Come on, pal," he said into the trees. "Let's get Cisco and get back to the ranch."

There was no reply, other than a muffled whimper. *He's got his fists in his mouth again,* Will thought.

"It's okay, pal," he said as he parted the branches. "I'm back. We're going home—"

But the words died on his lips. There in front of him was Abe, his hands and feet tied and a rag stuffed into his mouth. His big gray eyes were wild with terror.

"What the devil?" Will said as he leaned toward him.

But that was as far as he got. He felt something sharp hit his head, just before the world went black.

✝ ⚜ ✝

Chapter Seventeen

*W*hen Will opened his eyes, everything was still black. But he knew right away it wasn't the black of ordinary night. It was a thick, inky darkness that was somehow familiar. In a spasm of terror, he put out his hand, and his fingers touched something hard and cold. He felt his way along it, and he found nothing but more hardness, more coldness, more darkness. He knew where he was.

He was back at the bottom of the mine shaft.

"Help!" he cried out. "Somebody help me!"

Just as they had the last time, the words only echoed in the deep cave, taunting him as they bounced off the walls and came back in his face.

It's not my own fault this time, he thought as he put his hands over his ears. *I didn't just fall in. But how did I get here?*

He tried to stand up, but pain shot through the back of his head, bringing the memory with it. Someone had hit him, just as he was about to—

"Abe!" he cried—and then he slapped his hand over his

mouth. It had to be the same person who tied Abe up and then conked Will himself over the head and dumped him here.

If he hears me, he thought, *he might come back and—finish the job.*

It wasn't a comforting thought, and the image of someone hurting Abe wasn't either. Will squeezed his eyes shut to close it out, though it was so dark in the mine he could have saved himself the trouble.

Or was it?

Will remembered something—something from the last time he'd found himself here—and he managed to get to his feet so he could look up. Was it still there? Was there still a "bend" in the downward tunnel where a crack of light might come through?

Or had whoever knocked him out and dumped him here closed up the opening?

That thought kept him on his feet, pain or no pain, and had him clawing at the walls.

I have to get up there! he thought. *I have to get out of here before I suffocate!*

Calm down, simple head. There's enough air in there to last you for days if you'd shut up for 10 seconds.

It was as if Olive were right there beside him, and it calmed Will down. He leaned his forehead against the cool rock and tried to think—straight thoughts this time.

I got out of here before. It wasn't all Olive's doing. I remember working pretty hard at it, as a matter of fact. What did I do?

He closed his eyes again, this time to imagine himself, rope tied around his waist, wedging himself between the walls and moving first his feet and then his shoulders.

I had a rope, though—

I'll do it without the rope, Olive had said.

"I told her I could, too," Will whispered. "I know I could have. I know I *can!*"

Already breathing as if he'd climbed Mt. Everest, Will planted his upper back firmly against the wall behind him and then put up his feet, one at a time. Pretending that the rope was around his waist, and that Olive was on the narrow ledge, waiting for him, Will closed his eyes and began the climb.

I did most of it last time, he told himself. *She just had the rope around me in case I fell. But I'm not gonna fall, and even if I do—no—no ifs—I can do this.*

So he kept on until his body began to fold in the middle, which meant the tunnel was getting narrower. He was almost to the ledge.

And then it struck him: *What do I do when I get there?*

Olive had been there before, waiting to haul him up as he threw his leg over. She wasn't there this time. She'd never be there again. She hated him now for accusing her father of stealing cattle. Maybe her father was even the one who had thrown him down here. Maybe he was waiting at the top—

The thoughts were too much for Will. His shoulders weakened, and he could feel himself sliding back down the wall.

"No!" he cried out. "No—I won't fall! I gotta fight!"

The words ricocheted off the cave walls like bullets, but as they hit Will, they tightened his shoulders back up, and with it his resolve: *I can do this. I can fight this battle. God'll help me.*

"You will," Will whispered toward the opening. "I know You will."

Then clenching his teeth and holding himself tightly between the walls, Will reached out his hand and felt for the ledge. Even as he did, he could see a difference in the shades of darkness. Some of it was the wet blackness of the mine, but in the midst of it was a faint shaft of gray light. He clutched at it— and it was the ledge.

Will got as much of himself through the narrow hole as he could, so that his head, chest, and arms were out of the lower part of the tunnel and into the opening. With a heave and a prayer, he let go with his legs and wriggled his upper body into the opening. There was nothing to hang onto—he'd had Olive before—but Will dug his fingers in until he found a tiny crevice. It pinched his fingertips, but he wedged them in and then brought up one knee. With one painful scrape against a rock, he was suddenly up on the ledge, with the cavernous lower half of the mine shaft below him.

He sat for a minute, curled like a worm, and tried not to cry.

"We did it, God," he whispered. This time he could see the light coming through the main opening, weak, but enough to see by. There were stars winking down at him, and he could make out the shadows of a tree, dancing in the wind across the hole.

I'm just gonna rest for a second, he told himself, *and then I'm gonna climb the rest of the way. I can do this. Thank You, God, for letting Olive teach me how to do that.*

He did cry then—just a few hot tears. And then he shook his head. He couldn't think about her now. He had to get out of here, and he had to find Abe. And he had to tell Mr. Tarantino—Olive or no Olive. This was a battle the kids couldn't fight alone.

He was just beginning to turn himself around to get into the best possible position for climbing to the top when he heard male voices growing louder outside the opening.

"I don't think you oughta do this," one voice said. "She looks familiar to me."

Will knew he had never heard the voice before. It was too high-pitched and whiney to be Olive's father.

"Of course she looks familiar, bonehead. She's one of them kids we knocked off their horses."

Will caught his breath and held it—hard. He knew that voice.

It had the feel of gravel to it. It sounded just like the man who had—

Knocked him from his horse.

"Naw—that ain't her," Whiney Voice said. "Girl I knocked off was little—a little Indian squaw."

"Look, we got the other two—now we got the girl. They're the only ones seen us. Tie her up, throw her in there, and let's get goin'."

"Fernandez seen us."

Gravel Voice gave a grunt. "'Course he seen us. We're supplyin' him, ain't we? But he don't know we're stealin' 'em, and besides, who's he gonna tell? He wants to live up here like a hermit with his kid, remember? Every patriotic citizen of Santa Fe would just as soon shoot the yella coward as look at him. Now c'mon—get the rope around her and dump her in the shaft."

"What if somebody comes lookin' for the kids, though? And what if them kids is screamin' for help?"

"You want I should finish her off first?"

"No!" Whiney Voice cried—with Will nearly crying out with him. "It's just that it's supposed to look like a accident, so how come we're tyin' her up? Why don't we just dump her in like we done the boy?"

"Yer never satisfied, are ya? She looks feistier than the kid. *If* she should come to down there, she could probably get out on her own."

"And then she'll tell!"

"Now do you want a real murder on your head, or are you gonna dump her like I told ya to?"

There was a long pause, and Will could picture the men, one of them cross-eyed, tying up an unconscious Olive. She had to be unconscious, or she would have been giving both of them a run for their money.

But Will hoped she wouldn't wake up. If they tossed her in

the mine shaft, he could wait until they were gone and get both of them out.

Above, Whiney Voice started up again. "I still don't know. She's older'n that little squaw I knocked down—and that other kid we tied up a while ago? The big dumb one? I *know* he wasn't one of the three of 'em."

"For the love o' Pete!" Gravel Voice snapped. "I'll do it myself—hey!"

There was a heavy thud, and then the sound of footsteps running away. Will looked up and choked on his own horror.

An arm hung down into the shaft.

For a minute all Will could do was gasp over and over. Was that Olive's arm? No—even in the dim light he could tell it belonged to a man. Had one of those guys killed the other one? Was his arm . . . still attached to his body?

Don't be stupid, Will scolded himself. *They're cattle rustlers, not butchers!*

Once he could stop choking on his own thoughts, his mind began to clear. The important thing, he knew, was that Olive was probably still lying up there unconscious. He had to get to her before this man woke up—*if* he woke up.

Will stifled a shudder and wedged himself between the walls. They were softer up here, where the rains could get to them now and then. He decided that was a good thing; that he could dig his feet in instead of letting them slide as they had on the hard-packed dirt and rock in the lower half. Then, remembering how easy Olive had made it look that day, he began to work his way upward.

It only took a minute for him to get to where the man's hand dangled before his face. Gingerly, Will touched it. It wasn't cold or stiff, and although he didn't know how long it took for a dead man to turn into a corpse, he decided it was because he was still alive.

That could be a good thing or a bad thing, he told himself. *I don't particularly want to see a dead guy—but he could also wake up and—*

He couldn't afford to think that thought. Setting his jaw, he inched his way past the arm and up almost to the opening.

"Okay," he whispered. "Heave ho!"

Keeping his feet dug into the wall, Will pushed his upper body out of the opening. As soon as his chest hit the ground, he crawled toward the out-cold man, who groaned.

Will looked around frantically for the other man. He had heard a thud and someone running away. Had the other man hit this one over the head before he ran? *That must be it,* Will thought. *The whiney-voice guy musta got scared. I bet he high-tailed it outa here.*

Once again, Will looked around, and what he saw made him want to yell in terror. He scrambled up, hand to his mouth. There at his feet, right next to the unconscious man, was Olive—eyes closed, with a rope tied around her arms and legs.

Without stopping to argue with himself, Will quickly untied the rope and scooped her up, flinging her over his shoulder. To his relief she felt warm as he stumbled away from the man on the ground, her unconscious weight heavy on his shoulder, her arms dangling against his back.

He had only gone about 10 yards when the man moaned again, and Will slipped behind the nearest pile of rocks with Olive still over his shoulder. He tried not to let his breathing be heard, though he was sure anyone within a hundred-mile radius could hear his heart beating. There was no more moaning from the direction of the mine shaft, so Will set Olive carefully on the ground—or at least he tried to.

There was somebody already there.

Will nearly dropped Olive as he jumped and choked back a scream. Whoever it was gave a muffled cry.

"Abe?" Will whispered. "Abe—is it you, pal?"

Carefully setting Olive down, Will knelt beside the crying form. It was Abe, all right, still bound and gagged and wild-eyed.

Will got close to his face, so that their noses were nearly touching.

"It's me, Abe," he whispered. "I'm gonna take this gag out of your mouth, but you can't make a sound. Promise?"

Abe nodded, though he was still whimpering behind his gag.

"Come on—you have to be absolutely quiet," Will whispered.

Abe nodded again, and his whimpering ceased. Slowly Will pulled the rag out of his mouth. Putting his fingers to his lips to remind him, Will then pulled off the ropes around his wrists and ankles. It wasn't hard to do. Abe could have gotten himself untied with one yank—but he had obviously been far too terrified.

They probably told him not to move or they'd do him in or something, Will thought. Right now, he wouldn't have put it past them.

But there was no time to ask Abe questions. They had to get back to the ranch before the bandit who was now unconscious at the mouth of the mine shaft came to.

Will motioned for Abe to pick up Olive, but then he put his hand on the boy's arm and listened. There were unsteady foot-steps, and then a heavy thud. Will kept listening, while Abe nearly crammed his own fist down his throat, but the night was quiet again.

Soundlessly, Will peeked around the rock. The man at the mine shaft had evidently come to, but he hadn't gotten far. Still, if he woke up again, right there, he was bound to see them.

"Come on," Will whispered over his shoulder. "Get Olive."

But Abe didn't have to be told. He was already cradling Olive in his arms, and he wasn't going to let Will out of his sight again. Holding his breath, Will slipped out from behind the rocks and crept, bent at the waist, through the gray darkness with Abe on his heels.

Even as he felt his way along, Will decided where to go. He wanted to go back to the ranch, but with Olive unconscious for this long, he had to get her to the closest place—and the closest place was her father's shack. He might be mad, but this was his kid. Surely he would take care of her—

Will couldn't think of any other way. Olive herself had said he was crazy sometimes, but he wasn't a thief—and the bandits had said as much themselves. He didn't know Olive's last name, but the "Fernandez" the two cattle rustlers had been talking about had to be her father, and if he was, he was buying stolen cattle without even knowing it. He was going to have to apologize to her—if he ever got the chance.

As they climbed the last hill before the shack, Will looked back to see how Abe was doing. He was barely breathing hard as he held Olive like she was a china doll. It made Will's heart lurch to see it, and he faced forward and moved faster. They were too far away for the bandit to hear them now.

By the time they reached the shack, Will himself was gasping for air, and his side felt as if it were ready to split open. He could feel the fight going out of him, and as he slowed his steps, he knew he wasn't going to get it back. There sat her father on the porch—with a gun across his lap.

✝ ⊹ ✝

Chapter Eighteen

*D*ear God, Will prayed in his head, *I can't fight anymore, but I don't wanna give up. What do I do? Please show me what to do!*

There was no time to wait for an answer. Olive's father stood up and peered into the darkness. He was wearing a white undershirt with straps, and Will could see it going up and down as he breathed, as if he'd been running. Slowly he raised the gun and aimed it—right at Will.

"No! Mr. Fernandez!" Will shouted. "We have Olive!"

The gun at once clattered to the porch floor, and Olive's father tore toward them. Abe pulled Olive up to his chest and hunched his shoulders, and when Mr. Fernandez got to them, Abe turned his back and whimpered.

"Take her inside, Abe," Will said. "It's all right—he'll take care of her."

Still eyeing Mr. Fernandez warily, Abe stumbled past him and carried his armful of Olive into the shack. Will turned to explain to the man, but he was right on Abe's trail, shooing him with his hands and barking orders at him. Will knew he was going to have a hard time getting Abe to let go of her once they were in there, and he was steeling himself for the argument as he followed them inside. The minute he crossed the threshold, however, he stopped cold.

There, lying on a bare mattress on the floor, was Mr. Tarantino, bound and gagged, just the way Will had found Abe.

"Mr. T.!" he cried.

Without a glance at Mr. Fernandez—who was already kneeling beside another mattress with Olive—Will flung himself down next to Mr. T. and yanked out the gag and started to work on the ropes. These were tied tighter than Abe's had been, and Will's fingers shook as he fumbled with them.

"I have never been so glad to see anyone in my life," Mr. T. murmured to him. His eyes were on Mr. Fernandez, who for the time being at least could only concentrate on Olive.

"Is the girl all right?" Mr. T. said, his voice still low.

"I don't know," Will whispered. "She's alive, but she's been out a while. I think they hit her over the head. That's what they did to me."

"Are you—"

"I'm fine." Will glanced over his shoulder. Abe was on one side of Olive, her father on the other. He and Mr. T. could probably have squeezed their way out the door of the crowded shack and neither of them would have noticed. Instead, Will leaned closer to Mr. T.

"What's going on?" he whispered. "How'd you get here—all tied up?"

"The ranch hands and I discovered more cattle missing, so we split up to look for the rustlers in earnest. I spotted them and followed them—not knowing *they* were following *her*."

"Her name's Olive," Will said.

"I know that now, but she's changed a great deal since I last saw her."

Will gaped at him. "You know her?"

"I've known her ever since she was a baby. Her father and I were colleagues." Mr. T. shook his head. "It's a shame. Anyway, I got in too close, thinking I could rescue the girl—Olive—and they got me. I let my guard down."

"But why did they bring you here?" Will said.

"They told Eduardo—"

Will pointed to Olive's father.

"Right," Mr. T. said. "They told him I had kidnapped his daughter and that my accomplices were going to come for the ransom. They said he'd better pay it, or everybody in Santa Fe would know where he was and there would be a lynch mob out here. The poor man is half out of his head from losing his wife and living out here all this time—he believed them. He's been sitting on that porch with his gun, waiting for my 'accomplices.'"

"He thought we were them," Will said. "It looked like he was gonna shoot us!"

"The Eduardo Fernandez I knew wouldn't kill a spider. I doubt the gun is even loaded."

Suddenly there were footsteps on the porch. Eduardo Fernandez didn't even look up from Olive's bed as two of Mr. T.'s ranch hands squirmed into the doorway, guns drawn.

"You can put those away," Mr. T. said. "I sure hope you brought horses."

"Horses!" Will cried.

Mr. T. looked at him, one eyebrow cocked.

"I've lost Cisco!" Will said.

"No you haven't," said the ranch hand with red hair and a face full of freckles. "He came home whinnyin' for his supper. Gabby's feedin' him."

Mr. T.'s probably never gonna let me ride again—or Señora

Otero either, Will thought. But there was no time for that right now. It took himself, Mr. T., and both of the ranch hands, all crammed together in the shack like pickles in a jar, to pry Mr. Fernandez *and* Abe away from Olive in order to get her on a horse with Mr. T. and get her to the ranch. Red rode on ahead to call a doctor and to send more hands back with mounts for Olive's father, Will, and Abe. The other hand, whose name, Will remembered, was Walt, stood on the front porch, just in case the rustlers came back.

One of them did, but not alone. Gabby galloped up on Cisco, with the bandit tied, gagged, and flung over Cisco's flanks like a sack of potatoes. *Rotten* potatoes, as far as Will was concerned.

"The fool came to the ranch wantin' help," Gabby said. "Told me he'd been beaned on the head by a cattle rustler. I got a little suspicious, though. So after Red showed up sayin' you were out here, I decided to bring him, hopin' you could tell me if this was one of 'em you seen that night."

Will went over to the man and crouched down to get a look at his eyes. "That's him, all right," he said. "I'd know those cross-eyes anywhere."

That was evidently a sore spot with the bandit, because he wriggled like a caught snake and screamed into his gag until his face turned purple.

"You know something?" Will said to him. "You really gotta learn to choose your battles. Some of 'em you just can't win."

It was a funny thing, Will decided as the next few weeks passed. Some chunks of time just dragged on with nothing happening in them but the dull day-to-day—and then others whipped past like speeding trains, loaded with events.

A day or two after the night-to-remember—as Mom named it, once she got over being furious with Will for not telling her about Olive in the first place and decided she actually understood—Mr. T. had Eduardo Fernandez checked into St. Vincent's Sanitarium and sold some of his recovered cattle to pay for his stay. He promised Eduardo he would take care of Olive, who was recovering nicely from her concussion and couldn't wait to be allowed out of bed. Mr. T. got busy converting an old outbuilding into a cottage for Señora Otero and Olive, so that the Señora could be there all the time to help with Olive's care, as well as keep Mr. T.'s house. That plan didn't bother Miguel a bit. He got to sleep in a bedroom in the main house.

Not long after that was the social studies exhibition at school. Will and Miguel won second prize. Mrs. Rodriguez told them they would have won first if they had managed to find a piece of raw turquoise to put in their model. Neither of them told her they *had* found one—but they'd given it to Olive while she was in the hospital. She said she'd treasure it forever. It made Will feel as if he *had* won first prize.

On April 29, Bud and Tina finally returned from Washington, and Abe was so happy to see them when they got off the train at Lamy, he just kept running from one to the other, covering Tina's face with kisses, and then lunging back to Bud to kiss his. Will thought it was a pretty embarrassing display, but Fawn commented that it was "sweet."

Ugh. She really *was* turning into a girl.

Bud and Tina were the center of attention for a whole day as they told about finally getting the official adoption papers for Abe—which they celebrated with a party in the Hutchinsons' backyard. But they had sad news as well. That was always the way, Will thought. They were only able to make the adoption final when they found out for certain that both of Abe's parents had been placed in Nazi concentration camps years before and had died there. American soldiers, they said, had been there and seen the horror.

"So it's true," Mom said. "There really were such horrible things."

Bud nodded, tears in his pale eyes. "We went to a conference headed by Edward R. Murrow. He had just returned from Germany and Poland. He said there are no words for the horror he saw." He gave a soft snort. "Of course, the Germans say they knew nothing about them, and those who were in charge of the camps said they were only obeying orders."

"Hitler's orders," Mr. T. said.

Bud nodded, his eyes sadder than Will had ever seen them. "As a pastor, I don't say such things lightly," he said. "But there is no punishment too harsh for that man."

The next day, Will decided it was as if Adolf Hitler knew that millions of people felt the same way. The news came that Hitler had committed suicide.

"It won't be long now, Will," his mother said that night.

She was sitting on the edge of his bed. It had been a long time since she had tucked him in, but tonight, without even talking about it, they both seemed to know that it was right. With Abe gone, his room was lonely and empty, and they could both feel change in the air.

"You really think the war's almost over, Mom?" Will said.

She looked surprised. "You're always the one who's telling *me* that," she said. "You're not giving up, are you?"

Will shook his head. "No. I'm just trying not to fight battles I don't have any control over. I'm letting God take care of this one."

"You know what that is, don't you?" Mom said.

"You mean, what it's called?"

"Uh-huh."

"No, what's it called?"

"It's called turning the other cheek," she said. "And I think you do it very well."

About a week later, Will was out at the ranch, playing checkers with Olive, who, although she was now allowed to sit up in a chair, announced that she was going to go absolutely crackers if they didn't let her get outside and run around soon.

"You have had a serious head injury," Señora Otero told her. She set down a tray with two glasses of cherry soda and two sopapillas which Will suspected were stuffed with whipped cream. "If you go back to your activities too soon, you will be back in bed for even longer."

"Never mind, then!" Olive wailed. "But how soon 'til I can go out?"

"In time," Señora Otero said, patting her hand. "In time."

She gave Will a knowing smile before she went back to the kitchen. Will decided that he was going to tell her all about everything he'd learned over the past few weeks, the first chance he got. Meanwhile, he had to keep Olive out of trouble.

"You're a terrible patient," Will told her.

"Thank you very much!"

"You need to learn how to choose your battles. Surrender once in a while."

She wrinkled her nose at him. "Know-it-all," she said. "Whose turn is it?"

"Yours."

Olive studied the board, as if the next move were crucial to her survival. "By the way," she said, almost absently, "I never did thank you for saving my life."

Will felt his eyebrows going up, but he didn't dare make a big deal out of it. He was getting to know Olive pretty well. Well enough to call her one of his best friends.

"So I guess that makes us even, huh?" he said.

"Not quite," she said. "You still have to make up for almost running me down with your horse that day."

"Don't you ever forget anything?" Will said.

Mr. T. came in just then from his study, and the look on his face put Will's current debate with Olive right out of his mind.

"Is everything all right?" Will said.

"It is very all right," Mr. T. said. But his usually tan face was white, and he sank into a chair near them.

"Are you sure?" Olive said. "Do you need some water?"

Mr. T. shook his head. "Germany just surrendered—unconditionally—to the Allies." He looked at them as if he barely knew them. "The war in Europe is over."

And then he put one hand on Will's shoulder and the other on Olive's. No one said a word.

But the next day, plenty was said. It was a day of celebration, and once more school was closed and business came to a halt in Santa Fe, but this time for a happier reason.

The church held a prayer service, complete with candles and glorious music. Will sat in a pew with his mother and Fawn, Tina and Abe, Mr. T. and Olive, and Señora Otero and Miguel and even Uncle José. There was barely room for all of them, and as it was Gabby and Red and the rest had to sit behind them.

"Shouldn't they be watching the cattle?" Will whispered to Mr. T.

He shook his head. "The other rustler was caught down near Golden this morning. Sheriff called to tell me." He smiled. Will smiled back. It was as if a lot of chapters were closing for good.

During the service, they all gave thanks for the victory in Europe and what it was going to mean to so many people. Will wondered if this meant that Fawn's father would be coming home soon, but he didn't mention it. Mom said it was better not to get Fawn too excited too soon, or there would be no living with her.

But they also prayed that there would be a victory just as complete in the Pacific, and that it would come soon.

I know it will, God, Will prayed as the congregation sang

"The Battle Hymn of the Republic" and the women—and some of the men—cried. *I'm not so angry anymore about it, but we've waited so long. Please, please, please make it happen.*

After church, they all piled into the Pink Adobe for a celebration dinner before heading for the planned "hoo-ha," as Mr. T. called it, in the Plaza. As a band began to play on the new bandstand that had quickly been constructed just for this night, and firecrackers popped from every rooftop, Will clutched his miniature flag in his hand and found Mr. T.

"I see a question sitting right on the tip of your brain," Mr. T. said when he saw him. "Fire away."

"I figured something out," Will said. "Sometimes when you don't fight—when you have to turn the other cheek—you win anyway."

"There is victory in surrender," Mr. T. said. "Good job, Will."

"So I guess you always win when you fight when God wants you to fight and you leave it to Him when He's the only one who can do the work."

The look Mr. T. gave him was soft. "I'm proud of you," he said. "I look forward to the day when I can tell your father that."

"But how do you know the difference? How do you know for sure when God wants you to fight and when He wants you to let Him do it? It seems like I make a lot of mistakes."

Mr. T. put his arm around Will's shoulders, in a man-to-man way that made Will swell out his chest.

"It takes a lifetime to learn that," Mr. T. said. "A lifetime of prayer and getting to know your Lord and making mistakes and being forgiven." He stopped and pointed to the little knot of kids in front of them, Abe and Miguel and Fawn and Olive and even Neddie. "This war was fought for all of you, you know. So you can all have the freedom to live that life I'm talking about."

Will thought about that. As the bells of St. Francis pealed endlessly and the crowds of people shouted in rowdy, good-natured

Spanish from the balconies of the LaFonda Hotel, Will closed his eyes.

I promise I'll live that kind of life, God, he prayed. *I'll live it for my dad.*

I'll live it for You.

☩ ⬥ ☩ ⬥ ☩

There's More Adventure in the
CHRISTIAN HERITAGE SERIES!

The Salem Years, 1689–1691

The Rescue #1
The Stowaway #2
The Guardian #3
The Accused #4
The Samaritan #5
The Secret #6

The Williamsburg Years, 1780–1781

The Rebel #1
The Thief #2
The Burden #3
The Prisoner #4
The Invasion #5
The Battle #6

The Charleston Years, 1860–1861

The Misfit #1
The Ally #2
The Threat #3
The Trap #4
The Hostage #5
The Escape #6

The Chicago Years, 1928–1929

The Trick #1
The Chase #2
The Capture #3
The Stunt #4
The Caper #5
The Pursuit #6

The Santa Fe Years, 1944–1945

The Discovery #1
The Mirage #2
The Stand #3
The Mission #4
The Struggle #5
The Choice #6